DARK NEEDS

DARK NEEDS
A Masked Man Dark Romance

C. Cyan

Dragonfly Hill Books, LLC

Copyright ©2024 by Dragonfly Hill Books, LLC

All rights reserved.

No portion of this book may be reproduced in any form without written permission from the publisher or author, except as permitted by U.S. copyright law. This is a work of fiction. Names, characters, places, and incidents are either the product of the author's imagination or are used fictitiously.

Paperback ISBN: 978-1-952898-19-8

CONTENTS

Foreword   1

From the Author   2

PART 1   4

Prologue   5

1. Chapter 1   7
2. Chapter 2   13
3. Chapter 3   19
4. Chapter 4   25
5. Chapter 5   29
6. Chapter 6   32
7. Chapter 7   37
8. Chapter 8   41

9.	Chapter 9	49
10.	Chapter 10	53
11.	Chapter 11	58
12.	Chapter 12	61
13.	Chapter 13	65
14.	Chapter 14	70
15.	Chapter 15	74
16.	Chapter 16	78
17.	Chapter 17	83
18.	Chapter 18	88
19.	Chapter 19	95
20.	Chapter 20	107
21.	Chapter 21	111
22.	Chapter 22	115
23.	Chapter 23	119
PART 2		127
24.	Chapter 24	128
25.	Chapter 25	138
26.	Chapter 26	144

27. Chapter 27	150
28. Chapter 28	154
29. Chapter 29	157
30. Chapter 30	166
31. Chapter 31	170
32. Chapter 32	178
33. Chapter 33	183
34. Chapter 34	191
35. Chapter 35	195
36. Chapter 36	200
37. Chapter 37	206
Epilogue	213
Content Warnings	216
Afterword	218

FOREWORD

This is a novel with dark themes. This thriller depicts a dark, unconventional romance and contains themes that aren't to everyone's liking. Please check the content warnings at the back of the book before reading. I have added them for those who might need them, but I wanted them at the end so that those who choose not to read them or who want to be surprised by the natural flow of events within the plot won't accidentally read them when trying to navigate to the beginning of the story.

FROM THE AUTHOR

Dear Reader:

I write darker romances with morally gray characters, questionable themes, and horror, which can be upsetting to some readers. I trust you know your triggers before you proceed.

If you are familiar with Mary Shelley's *Frankenstein; or, the Modern Prometheus*, you may recognize some similarities between the monster and Travis. This is intentional, as I wanted to pay homage to the original story. And thus, Justin is Victor in this tale; he made the monster, and the monster will make him pay for abandoning him. You may see some other parallels in this reimagining of *Frankenstein*, but if you are familiar with the classic novel, rest assured that this is a very different, modern, and fresh story.

SN: It was probably the first novel I read as a young college student that made me think, "If she could write such a killer story at 18, so can I!" And horror, at that! I was also 18 at the time, and this was back when gatekeepers kept so much talent from realizing their dreams, so it would be another twenty years before I published my first book. But Mary Shelley remained my author role model for a long time. There are also a few nods to *The Phantom of the Opera* within this novel for those of you who love that story.

Enjoy.

C. Cyan

PART I

"Beware; for I am fearless, and therefore powerful."
 "I have love in me the likes of which you can scarcely imagine and rage the likes of which you would not believe. If I cannot satisfy the one, I will indulge the other."
 - Mary Shelley, *Frankenstein*

PROLOGUE

I have an intense amount of hatred for humankind, but my handsome face conceals my evil thoughts and my nefarious intentions. Appearance can cover a multitude of sins. So can money, and I have plenty of that, too.

In my wicked deeds, I find power.

At only twelve, I watched a girl drown in the river. And I *liked* it. It was thrilling and intimate in a way that I never expected death to be. As she sank down into the water and rose again, she reached for me, pleading with wide eyes full of fear and hope for me to save her. I watched her hope melt away as she fought the current. I had the power to save her or watch her die. By the time the current pulled her under, I was hard from exhilaration, so I had to deal with that before putting on a surprisingly convincing show for the police.

After that experience, I went down a rabbit hole—visiting dark websites that showed me way more than my young brain was prepared for, but it was a dopamine rush every time I saw someone tied up and used. I liked it. I craved it. I couldn't wait until I was old enough to do those things to another human being.

The human body is both delicate and can take so much abuse. That fascinates me as much as death mesmerizes me.

At sixteen, other boys got their first car and utilized the backseat with some little virginal thing or scored alcohol or coke and went to parties. I, on the other hand, thought I was old enough to turn some of my dark fantasies into reality. My father caught me with a twenty-year-old I'd promised the world to—and who was gullible enough to believe me. I'd tied her up and defiled her, but I hadn't gotten to do what I wanted with her when my father interrupted. He paid a hefty sum to her to keep her quiet.

I had plenty of girlfriends in between my experiments, but I didn't really treat them much better. When a person doesn't value life, it's difficult to keep up the façade of infatuation for long. Mostly, I felt apathy toward those girlfriends, and they were only a means to an end—for sex and status.

Now, I've learned to be extremely selective about my pursuits, and I take my time understanding a person's weaknesses. It's almost a science, which my scientific mind enjoys. For instance, I've found that it's much harder to break the spirit of a prostitute than a woman from a "good" background. They're too easy, but a prostitute puts up a fight. I can toy with one three times longer than I can with other women. More time means more satisfaction for me.

Other than that, their backgrounds don't matter to me.

The only thing that matters is the thrill of attending to my dark needs.

CHAPTER 1

Kenzie Cameron felt the warm October sun through the window, but she stayed in bed, blowing away a tendril of blonde hair from her face before opening her eyes. She hated getting up on Friday mornings. Okay, she hated getting up *any* morning when it was chilly in the house, though she was never a bounce-out-of-bed-at-sunrise kind of girl, even when it was warm inside.

The night before, she worked late at Jameson's Haunted Farm and Spook Trail, so it was almost 2 AM before she showered and hit her pillow. Besides, she had another sex dream about her crush, fellow college sophomore Justin Reese Greyer, so she was reluctant to stop the fantasy.

Fuck, the dream was hot. He'd been right in the middle of screwing her from behind when she woke to the sounds of her roommate making breakfast. She squeezed her legs together against the returning pulsation in her pussy at the mere thought of his cock inside her.

Not that she knew what his cock was like. She'd been interested in him for months, but he hadn't made a move on her. Kenzie sighed. She'd tried to make her interest in him obvious, but he seemed so unattainable. He was one of those golden boys on campus—rich, smart, and popular. And he looked like one of her favorite actors, so in her mind, Justin was the complete package.

She moved her fingers to her panties. Soaked, just as she guessed they'd be. She swirled two fingers over the moist fabric and felt a jolt of need deep inside her core. She needed an orgasm to shake her this morning, and if Justin's dick couldn't do it, her fingers would have to. Kenzie closed her eyes, pressed harder against her clit through her wet panties, and imagined Justin ramming into her from behind, just like in her dream.

In her fantasy, he says, "Damn, Kenzie, your hole is tight tonight," his voice raspy with desire and his breath is hot against her ear. He leans into her, yanks up her shirt and bralette, and gropes her tits with both hands.

Kenzie swiped a fingertip over her hard nipple as her other hand massaged her pussy, but her mind wandered to Jameson Farm, imagining Justin finally admitting how hot she makes him.

"Mm hmm," she murmured. Kenzie slipped her fingers down the front of her panties, her hips moving to the motions of her daydream, her pussy saturated and hot. She spread her legs wider as her fingertips circled her clit, and then she plunged two fingers into her slippery hole, over and over as she imagined his cock filling her up. Kenzie threw her head back against her pillow as she imagined Justin pulling her hair toward him so that he could nibble at her throat. She loves biting, and he knows it. At least, in this fantasy, he does.

His teeth graze her neck and then bite into her shoulder. It's animalistic, and it's just hot enough that her insides clench in response. In the fantasy, Justin comes inside her pussy with an agonizing groan of pleasure. She loves the thought of his hot cum dripping from her pussy lips when he pulls out.

Still in bed, Kenzie bit back a scream of pleasure as her pussy clenched her fingers in an orgasm. She rode it as long as she could before her eyes fluttered open. Kenzie gasped when she saw movement to her right and realized she had an audience. "The fuck?"

"I should have woken up like *you* this morning." Kenzie's roommate, Lena Fitzgerald, leaned against the open doorway, her long dark hair in a messy bun on the top of her head, tendrils hanging down from sleep. She wore the shortest shorts possible, and Kenzie saw how hard her nipples were in the tight t-shirt she had worn to bed the night before.

"Boundaries, Lena!" Kenzie said as she tossed a pillow at Lena's smirk.

"There's no way *not* to hear it with these thin walls," Lena pointed out.

"I had an amazing dream about Justin again." Kenzie closed her eyes for a moment and bit her bottom lip.

"Eh, you could do better than him."

"He's literally the man of my dreams, Lena. Almost six-foot tall, svelte, deep voice, and brown eyes I could get lost in. And I'm going to make him mine before this semester is over."

"I guess the fact that he's a rich frat boy doesn't hurt, huh?" Lena crossed her arms. "What about love?"

Kenzie didn't have much growing up. They hadn't been living in poverty, but as a teen, she realized her parents lived paycheck to paycheck. There wasn't extra. Of course, money mattered. It only didn't matter to those who had more than enough of it. And love? Kenzie's parents flashed into her mind—a man who cared more about drinking than about living, and a woman who also gave up on living, in her resigned way.

"What about it? It just creates a bunch of misery," Kenzie replied.

Lena looked thoughtfully out Kenzie's window. "No. Love saves people from their own misery."

Ah, so Lena was a hopeless romantic. Maybe she hadn't seen how much a bad relationship can tear people down, how life can suck the light and the love from people. "Not for my parents. I don't even know why they're still married."

"I don't know your parents. But maybe it *was* real love." Lena gave her a look of pity. "Get your ass up and have some of these amazing waffles I slaved over this morning. You don't have to work at the student loan office today?" Lena turned and headed into the kitchen.

Kenzie threw off her covers, slipped into her blue bunny house shoes, and grabbed her robe. "No, I have the day off." She stopped in the bathroom, turned on the hot water in the shower, and took off her clothes. She pulled up her hair into a clip and stepped into the steam. Hot water thrummed against her skin, warming her almost instantly. She knew it wouldn't last long, so she lathered up.

Kenzie heard the bathroom door open. Lena had a bad habit of coming in whenever she wanted. Kenzie made a mental note to ask the super in their building to fix that door lock. At least Lena couldn't see into the shower stall with all the steam the hot water made.

"Are you working the creeper trail tonight?" Lena asked.

Lena hated the idea of Jameson's. It was a seasonal job that paid a decent amount of money, though, and to be honest, Kenzie freaking loved it. She'd grown up watching scary movies with her dad, and she loved reading horror novels when she wasn't inundated with required reading for her college coursework. Working a horror gig each autumn was perfect for her.

"Yep. And Justin is going to be there, too. He told me last night that he's wearing a brand-new costume, but he wouldn't tell me what. He wants me to guess who he is."

"Do I sense a little teasing on his part? Is he finally getting a clue?"

Kenzie grinned as she let the hot water massage her shoulders. The muscles deep in her core clenched again for a moment as she thought of him coming up on her in the darkness without even knowing it was him. Kenzie would love that. "I dunno. He said, 'I'll be watching you, and you won't even know it's me.' How hot is that?" She turned off the shower.

"Or weird and cringey?"

Kenzie stuck her head past the shower door and gave Lena an incredulous look. "Hot. *Definitely* hot. Justin Reese can stalk me any day." Kenzie turned off the water, grabbed her towel, dried off, and wrapped it around her torso. Sitting on the toilet lid, Lena was painting her fingernails purple when Kenzie stepped out of the shower. Lena had to swing her long legs to the side to give Kenzie room to brush her teeth at the sink in the small bathroom.

"Well, if he happens to sneak into this house and slips into my closet for a late-night stalker tryst, you better not toss his ass out."

Lena's arm brushed Kenzie's towel-covered thigh as Kenzie reached for the toothpaste in the cabinet above the sink. "Can't make any promises there."

"And just in case he wants to play in the dark tonight, I'm wearing that red pushup bra that defies gravity." Kenzie grinned devilishly and stuck her toothbrush in her mouth.

CHAPTER 2

Kenzie sprayed her shoulder-length blonde hair with so much hairspray, it stood straight out and up. Then she sprayed it with black hair color until only a platinum blonde streak on either side of her head zigzagged from each temple. She lined her face and jaw with black eyeliner and gave it the appearance of stitches with little Xs. With some theatrical makeup, she'd given her skin a pale, almost green tint, and she rimmed her eyes with dark shadow and lots of mascara. A bit of purple blush under her cheekbones accentuated them. She darkened her eyebrows and extended them out past their natural stopping point, giving them a sharp angle at the top. She finished the look with a dark red matte lipstick that would stay on most of the night.

Kenzie stepped back from the mirror and looked at her work with a critical eye. Yes, the Bride of Frankenstein was looking like a sinister monster snack. She gave herself a smile, satisfied that the image in the mirror looked deliciously deranged.

Kenzie grabbed her magical red bra and stuffed her breasts in it. She squeezed into a white leather bustier and put on a flowing white skirt over little red panties that matched the red bra. Recently, it seemed as if Justin had been flirting with her, so hopefully, she'd be able to show him the goodies hidden under her costume. After wrapping her arms in a white loosely netted gauze material she'd found online, Kenzie spritzed her decolletage with her favorite spicy perfume and grabbed her bag off her bed.

Lena was already at work, so the house was quiet, and the afternoon sun streamed in through the blinds in the front windows. Kenzie found comfort in the golden glow of October, where crisp, colorful leaves and bright orange pumpkins created a warmth no other season could match. It was warm now, but the chill of the October night would soon settle into her bones again. She hoped Justin could warm her from the inside out before dawn. Kenzie blew out a caramel apple-scented candle that Lena had left burning on the coffee table before she left.

Kenzie drove twenty minutes outside of town into the rolling hills of deep forests and vast brown fields where corn and cotton had already been harvested, leaving only jagged stalks. Last year, after a couple of years of bad weather, poor crops, and growing loans, Mr. Kenny Jameson opened the haunted attraction. He knew her dad and had offered her the job before he even advertised openings. At the time, she wasn't working for the student loans office, and she was desperate for some cash. Besides, it seemed like a fun way to spend her weekend nights. After watching her dad struggle with alcoholism, she didn't enjoy the club scene very much, so this was something different. It's where she'd first laid eyes on Justin Reese, but last fall, she didn't have the confidence to talk to him. It wasn't until he showed up in her Biology class this semester that she struck up a conversation with him.

Kenzie parked her car at the far end of the field where the other workers had parked. During the day, the Jamesons hosted a pumpkin patch that included a corn maze, a small playground with a corn pit, slides, tire swings, and lots of cutesy places to take pictures. Most of the families and small children left at dusk after buying hot apple cider and s'mores packets to make around the large fire pit near the entrance. She often passed kids with sticky fingers and satisfied bellies carrying pumpkins home to carve later. Teens and college kids rolled in after dusk to prove their bravery in the corn maze and spook trail.

Last year, Kenzie worked as a witch, jumping out of an old feed barn as people passed by, but it wasn't her favorite place to be because the clowns that ran out of the barn always took her glory. And fucking clowns creeped her out. She wasn't scared of much, but clowns were terrifying.

This year, she'd moved up to working as a character in the spook trail. Dressing as the Bride of Frankenstein was her idea. She'd wanted something sexier and more enticing since Justin Reese would probably be out there again this year.

It turned out that he loved horror films as much as she did. They'd had a few quick conversations in class about which movies were their favorites, but he hadn't invited her over to watch any with him. And she suspected he had a mean streak to want to scare kids all season. He sure didn't need the money.

The new sexy costume worked. The first night they worked together, Justin could barely peel his eyes away from her cleavage. She'd felt so powerful—as if she could bend his will with her sex appeal. Just thinking about him sent a puddle to her pussy. If she didn't fuck him soon, she'd lose her mind. She sighed. Maybe *he* was the one with all the power.

"Hi," said a tall, African American guy wearing a dark pair of coveralls and holding a plastic machete. His name was Derek, and he was new. He was stuck taking up money until sundown, which is when he'd take his place along the haunted trail to scare people. His hockey mask sat atop his head. He stared at her tits, which she poked out even more.

"Ready for lots of screams tonight?" Kenzie grinned.

He finally brought his dark eyes up to her face. "Always," he said suggestively, with a raised eyebrow. His hand instinctively went to his dick, which he pulled at.

Do I make your dick twitch? she wondered mischievously. Then, she chastised herself. She had no intentions of fucking Derek. It was all this damned pent-up horniness that had her acting so slutty. "Have fun, then," she replied. She really needed to spend more time with her vibrating toys, apparently. She smirked as she headed into the haunted attraction. Maybe the bride's secret was that she had a rabbit pulsing away inside of her through multiple orgasms. That'd make anyone look wild-eyed and electrified. Or maybe she was like Kenzie and hadn't had sex in *forever*. "Longest fucking dry spell ever," she muttered.

Kenzie's phone buzzed with a message, and she grinned when she saw it was from Justin.

> I'm watching you right now.

Her grin widened as she looked around. Lots of people moved about, many of them with masks on, so she had no idea from which direction Justin was watching her. The sheer thought of him watching her made her nipples hard, though. Was it the bigfoot making his way toward the haunted trail? Or was it the ghost in a bedsheet with eye holes cut out that seemed to be gliding toward the barn?

> Give me a hint?

> That wouldn't be as fun.

> Definitely ready for some fun. Join me when you get a chance?

> I've got something for you to taste.

> J: Licking my lips in anticipation.

Damn, she thought. *Fucking finally*. Her pussy throbbed, and she hoped he wouldn't wait too long. She liked this playful side of him. She passed through the entrance to the spook trail, with its giant iron spider, surrounded by a pile of orange, white, and yellow pumpkins and gourds. A gauzy spider web stretched every possible direction around the frame with the words "SPOOK TRAIL" and a warning underneath that read, "Turn back now!" Kenzie stuck her phone into the little bag she carried and made her way to her spot in the edge of the woods, where

C. CYAN

she waited for the darkening sky and the first visitors down the trail.

CHAPTER 3

Hearing screams up ahead, Kenzie smiled, giddy with bubbling anticipation about scaring the shit out of the next group of kids. They clambered clumsily along the path, crunching leaves as they walked. The jack-o'-lantern that she held cast eerie shadows across her face through the open top, and she knew her dark makeup made her look even scarier.

As they neared, their voices activated the strobe light in the tree overhead. She stepped around the huge oak and hissed at the group of teenagers as she grabbed at the group with one hand, her black nails narrowly missing them. Three girls stopped dead in their tracks; one yelped while another one cursed, and they backed into the two guys behind them. A fourth girl took off down the trail without her friends.

One of the guys, trying to maintain his macho status, grabbed his crotch and said, "Hey, want a snack?" He leered at the girls, who gave him frowns. He shrugged. "She's just hungry, is all."

The other guy with them laughed as one of the girls, a blonde in the shortest shorts possible and a cropped top, punched him in the arm, and they continued down the trail after the friend who'd run ahead.

Kenzie heard the chainsaw down the trail, and she snickered when she heard the group screaming as they ran from Rick, a linebacker for the college who loved chasing people down the trail with the chainsaw. Though it didn't have the chain on it, the loud noise scared just about everyone who went past him. He didn't even have to wear a mask. Rick showed up each evening in overalls with his hair spiked up all crazy and dark makeup smudged under his eyes. He looked like the epitome of a psycho redneck.

The closer it got to Halloween, the busier Jameson's Haunted Farm became. Tonight was no exception. Kenzie had been on her feet for most of four hours, and her toes hurt in her boots.

As the night wound down, groups came through less and less, so she took a seat on a hay bale to give her feet a rest. It was getting cold, and she wondered when Justin would show up. Maybe he'd ghosted her. She pouted. She held her hands over the small flame of the candle in her jack-o'-lantern for warmth. Her eyes watered from the wind whipping around the trees. The dry leaves overhead shuddered against the chilly breeze.

Kenzie stood and peeked around the oak to see if anyone was coming down the trail. Seeing no one, she turned but stopped in her tracks. From the dim light of the candle inside the pumpkin, she saw a man standing at the tree line. He held a long knife in one hand, and he wore a mask that looked like a scarecrow and a flannel shirt and jeans. Her heart jumped into her throat before she remembered Justin telling her he'd come find her later.

"Fuck, Justin Reese! You scared me." She let out a nervous laugh as the strobe light overhead activated. "I didn't even hear you walk up." She bent forward, taking her time to set down the jack-o'-lantern, giving him ample time to look at her tits in the candlelight's glow. Kenzie stood back up and leaned against the tree. "Are you gonna come warm me up or just stare at me all night?"

As the scarecrow cocked his head, she saw him tighten his grip on the knife. Was it real? It *looked* real, but Justin knew actual knives weren't allowed out here.

"You don't have to be shy with me. I want this. Come here."

The scarecrow moved toward her with slow, purposeful steps. When he was near her, she realized how tall he was. And big. Justin must have beefed up his costume to make himself look more menacing.

Without a word, he grabbed her by the neck and held her against the tree. Her eyes widened. She didn't know this was his kind of kink, but it sent a jolt of want straight to her core. "I've wanted this a long time," she whispered.

He tightened his grip on her throat, and her pussy reacted instinctively.

Then, he sniffed her. She heard him pulling in her scent and releasing it over and over. It was primitive and hot as fuck.

He raised the knife with his other hand and dragged the tip down her temple and cheek where she'd drawn the fake lines and stitches. She gasped at the coldness of the steel.

The knife *was* real.

Was Justin into kinky knife-play? He ran the tip along her neck, over her collarbone, and into the gulf between her breasts as she tried not to move or even breathe. It poked her tender skin but didn't pierce it.

This awakened a new level of sexual desire. Kenzie never thought she'd be into something like this, but with the blade against her skin, a thrill of heat coursed through her body from the metal all the way down to deep inside her stomach. She hadn't thought it was possible to get more excited than she was when he'd sniffed her. Wrong.

What if this wasn't Justin Reese? That tantalizing possibility sent a shiver through her. What if this was some deranged madman who had come to the spook trail to murder a bunch of people, and she was the first? The idea that it could be *anyone* thrilled her.

Had she watched too many horror movies? She was letting her imagination run away with her. Right?

Kenzie licked her lips as the fire in her belly grew. She was more ready than ever for Justin to be inside her. "Oh, that feels good," she mumbled, encouraging him. She closed her eyes, and her lips parted as her chest heaved with desire. Her whole body felt alive with electricity, and she truly felt like Frankenstein's bride. She wanted him to take her like the monster would take his bride on their wedding night—brutal sex, with raw desire that left her aching in the morning.

The scarecrow pressed closer to her, tightening his grip on her neck so much that she was getting lightheaded. She felt his cock hardening between them. Her hand went to it. She needed a sexual release of all the pent-up frustration, and the instrument of that release was right in front of her, begging to be used. She enveloped the bulge in his pants, rubbing up and down against the rough material. He let go of her neck, and she hadn't realized how hard he'd been gripping her until that moment. Cold replaced the warmth of his hand as air flooded back into her aching throat, and she coughed.

Kenzie saw the glint of his eyes in the mask. With his free hand, he pushed her to her knees, and she fumbled with his zipper until his cock sprang free. The skin was soft and warm, but it was rock hard in her hand—and longer than she imagined.

"Suck it," he said, his voice low and guttural.

Her stomach fluttered hearing Justin's voice, deep with desire for her. At first, she gently touched the tip with her tongue and then took the head into her mouth. She could hold the head of his dick in her mouth and still had room to hold the rest of it with both fists. Then she lapped at his cock, already tasting the saltiness of his precum. She picked up speed, wondering if he planned to shoot cum down her throat.

Kenzie smiled around him in her mouth. She was finally getting her chance with the big man on campus, and she planned on making Justin Reese's wildest fantasies come true.

He grabbed the back of her head and shoved it further into her mouth. Soon, he was fucking her mouth so hard, she could barely breathe or think straight. He shoved it deeper, making her gag, and then it was gone. He'd pulled out of her mouth, leaving only a string of saliva between them.

CHAPTER 4

The scarecrow threw her to the ground and wrestled with her skirt as he bent over her. She saw his hard cock bobbing in the light from the jack-o'-lantern, and she widened her legs to give him easy entrance. She was so wet and ready for him. With the knife, he cut her red panties. She cried out in protest. Those were her favorite pair, dammit.

A pinpoint of blood sprang up on her hip where the tip of the knife had pierced her skin in a shallow half-inch-long cut. The scarecrow smeared it with his finger and then plunged his finger into her wet pussy. His fingers were thick, and he soon plunged two, then three into her as if he was making sure she could accommodate his fat cock. She was so wet, she thought she could take two cocks inside her pussy at the moment, and she needed to be filled. Rocking her hips in time with the thrusts of his fingers, she writhed in ecstasy. She wanted him inside of her *now*.

"Fuck me, Scarecrow. Please," she rasped. "Fuck me hard."

The scarecrow paused and looked down at her for a few beats, and for a moment, she thought he was going to get up and leave her there in a writhing agony of horniness. He finally lowered himself onto her and slid his cock in. It still stretched her tight pussy, and she grasped his arms and threw her head back as he pushed all the way in. He hit bottom, that dull ache of a big dick filling her up, and she groaned.

Just then, she heard more people coming down the path. "Fuck," she muttered. The bales of hay obscured them, but she was still afraid customers might see the scarecrow pounding away at the undead bride's pussy. He didn't let up, though. She heard him grunting beneath the mask as he fucked her as hard and as fast as he could. She never in a million years would have guessed that Justin would be such a forceful or voyeuristic lover.

The people passed without seeming to notice their fucking. They were too intent on what might be up ahead, she guessed. Besides, by this time of night, the ones coming through were usually half drunk.

He yanked at the front of her dress so that one titty popped out of the bustier, and he pulled at the lacy red bra to free it. Her skin was alabaster in the moonlight and the dancing flame of the jack-o'-lantern. He paused, seemingly entranced by the sight of her dark areola. Then, he thumbed her nipple and squeezed her breast. His hands were rougher, too, than she'd expected. She couldn't think about it long, though, because her pussy clenched as she rode out an orgasm, her scream of ecstasy mixing with the screams of teenagers and college kids running from Rick with the chainsaw down the trail. The orgasm was long, and she kept her eyes shut as long as her pussy pulsed around his dick, trying to hold on to the euphoria for as long as she could.

When she opened her eyes, she noticed Justin had slowed to watch her climax. She saw the excited glint of his eyes through the mask holes.

Green eyes.

Kenzie blinked. Didn't Justin have brown eyes?

Her brain was mush after such an explosive orgasm. She must have imagined green eyes in the dim light of the candle in the jack-o'-lantern.

"Scarecrow," she said with a smile and drowsy eyes, "let me kiss you." She reached up to remove his mask, but he slammed her wrist down on the ground with his hand, sending a shock of pain through hers. She yelped.

He pulled out of her and twisted her over, pushing up her skirt so that her bare ass was in the air. He pulled her hips closer as he pushed his cock back into her pussy. This different angle hurt, but it was the good kind of pain that made her want more of it even as she winced from it. He held one hand on her hip and the other on the opposite shoulder, and he slammed into her pussy so fast and so hard, she was sure she'd be bleeding from the force of it before he was done. She was almost to the point that she couldn't take it anymore when he slammed into her once more. He cried out a guttural moan as he came inside her, which made the pain of it worth it. He filled her pussy with cum as he shot load after load inside her. When he pulled his dick out of her, she felt it dripping out. She was thankful she was on the shot.

"Fuck, Justin. Where did that come from?"

The scarecrow stood without a word, tucked his cock back into his pants, and picked up his knife. Apparently, Justin Reese was still playing the masked monster.

She turned over, too weak in the knees to stand. "Well, thank you," she said a bit timidly. "I'll be right here tomorrow night if you want a round two." She bit at her bottom lip as her eyes fluttered back to the bulge in his pants.

The scarecrow watched her for a moment longer and headed down the trail.

Kenzie sat in a daze, hot cum still dripping out of her pussy and into the dirt and dead leaves under her ass, when she heard another group of people coming down the trail. She pushed her titty back into her bra and bustier, stood, grabbed her jack-o'-lantern, and waited to scare the shit out of them.

CHAPTER 5

As he walked, he clenched his jaw. He hadn't found Justin Reese fucking-Greyer-the-motherfucking-third, but that was okay. He'd apparently found one of Justin's many sluts. A good revenge fuck was just what he'd needed. And he had to admit, she'd been a damn good piece of ass. And she'd loved it, too, thinking she was getting a good pounding by the frat boy. Nothing could've made it better—except for Justin walking up on him fucking the girl in the Bride of Frankenstein costume, seeing him make her come as she screamed in ecstasy. Her face, frozen in the throes of pleasure, haunted him, white in the moonlight, with scars drawn down each side as though Fate was taunting him. *See*, Fate said, *a girl as scarred as you are*. Though he knew her scars were only makeup.

It was as if Fate had dropped her right into his lap. Well, right onto his dick. He smirked as he made his way back to the mansion. He gripped the knife tighter, almost turning back around to find the fucking weasel among the costumed college kids running around the farm. God, he hated Justin.

He sighed and kept walking. No, it was too late tonight now that he'd wasted his time on the girl. Too few people were around. It needed to be when the entire farm was crawling with people in costumes. Justin's little girlfriend had bought him some more time. Because if she hadn't gotten into his path tonight, he'd have slit Justin's throat like he should have done a year ago.

If he didn't get to him soon, Justin would realize that his frat buddy was missing, and he might get suspicious. He wanted to take Justin by surprise when he finally watched the life die out of his beady fucking eyes.

He made his way slowly down a ravine and back up the other side. Anyone else would have gotten hopelessly lost or injured in these woods, but he'd grown up here. Before his parents died, he spent many happy days running wild and free in the woods on their 220 acres, and he knew the land by heart, even in the dark of night. Jameson had offered to buy up some of it after his parents died, but he'd refused to sell. He hadn't needed the money, and the land and sprawling house were the only things he had left of the fond memories of his childhood—of the time when his family was still whole and happy.

The trees thinned out as he neared the old well, which had been on the property long before his father had bought the place in the 90s. It'd been long out of use and covered. In the moonlight, the stones shined like a forgotten pagan shrine. Two-hundred feet down it, a body lay at the bottom. He'd thrown Vaughn down there alive yesterday.

He caught the faint smell of the decomposing body through cracks in the wood that covered the top of the well and decided he'd better cover it with the lime he'd found in the barn left over from his father's short-lived experiment with farming. That should take care of the stink. He'd pour it down the well tonight and check on it again tomorrow. Maybe he'd mix up some cement, too, just to be sure. Lots of people would soon be looking for Vaughn Armstrong, considering his father was a state representative. They'd never find him out here, though. They wouldn't even know to look here. Even if they did, even if they brought a damn good cadaver dog that caught the scent, it'd be way too late. It'd all be over.

A twig snapped, and he turned around, gripping the knife tightly in his fist. He held his breath, listening. Surely, that stupid girl hadn't followed him. He hoped she hadn't because he didn't want to kill her.

He wasn't a murderer by nature. A chain of events had driven him to vengeance.

A deer raised its head about twenty yards away and stared at him before bounding off into the thicket. He let out a breath that wisped from his mouth like he was expelling a ghost from his lungs. If only. If only he could expel the hate and negative energy that burned and curled within him—the hate that made him do terrible things. He hated them for what they did to him physically, but even more, he hated them for the man they'd turned him into. The monster.

He headed toward the house. He was tired, but he had preparations to complete before he'd allow himself to rest.

CHAPTER 6

"It was the best fuck of my life." Kenzie sipped a beer. No wonder Justin was one of the most popular guys on campus. He probably had women throwing pussy at him left and right with skills like that. She pursed her lips as the cold beer went down her throat. That thought didn't really set well with Kenzie at the moment. "Seriously, I don't know how he could top it."

When she'd gotten home, she'd still been so horny that she'd plunged a vibrator into her still-wet and cum-soaked pussy to bring herself to another orgasm before she washed away his spunk in the shower.

"I wanna be fucked like that every day for the rest of my life. Seriously, I don't know if it was the costume, the knife, or his big dick that made it so good," she said as she squeezed her knees together against the twinge of desire she felt again between her legs. "I think I have a new kink, though. Who knew I'd like monster sex."

It was now just after midnight, and Lena had come in from her shift at the bar with a 12-pack of beer. Lena grinned. "Damn. Makes my jaunt with Chris in the storeroom at the bar seem tame in comparison." Chris was her boss, a 30-something tatted motorcycle guy. She'd been having sex with him for a few months, and Kenzie suspected her roommate was falling for him.

"The way he screwed me so effortlessly, just tossing me around and pounding away," Kenzie said as she bit her bottom lip and sighed. Kenzie and Lena giggled and clinked their beers together. She'd miss swapping sex stories and hanging out with Lena when she graduated. She could see herself being friends with Lena until they were old and gray, so she hoped their lives didn't take them too far away from each other.

The girls were tipsy. It didn't take Kenzie a lot to get there because she so rarely drank alcohol.

Just then, her phone vibrated where it rested between her legs, and she let out a yelp as it sent pulses across her tender clit. Both women fell into another fit of giggles. Kenzie glanced at her phone. "It's a text from Justin."

She pulled up her messages and read, a frown creasing her brow.

> *Sorry I couldn't get to you tonight.*
>
> *What do you mean?*
>
> *You weren't Scarecrow?*
>
> *What scarecrow?*

Kenzie gasped and put a hand over her mouth. "What?" Lena asked. "What did he say?"

Kenzie just shook her head. If Justin wasn't Scarecrow, who did she fuck on the spook trail?

Her shoulders relaxed. He was probably messing with her again. Kenzie rolled her eyes. "He's trying to make me believe it wasn't him out there tonight."

Yet... she thought about how broad-shouldered the guy had been, how tough his hands were, how deep his voice was, and how he had a real knife in his hand.

Lena took another swig of her beer, her eyelids heavy.

> Kenz, what scarecrow???

> I wasn't feeling well. I went home early.

> A scarecrow came to my station on the trail.

> I thought he was you.

> No, but he better not have kept you warm like I was planning to do.

Shit, she thought. She felt queasy as anxiety bubbled up in her stomach. Scarecrow could have been literally anyone.

Though, to be fair, she'd known there was the chance that Scarecrow wasn't her crush. A small part of her found that possibility incredibly hot—being fucked by someone completely random. She'd never done anything like that before, though. Out there in the woods, where everyone wore a costume, it would be easy for someone to act like someone else. Though, as she thought back, he never said he was Justin. He just didn't correct her when she'd called him by the name.

Green eyes.

Even as her heart raced from the fear and danger of being screwed by a stranger, she felt a deep pull of desire in her abdomen.

> Nobody could keep me warm like you.

She sent the last message to placate Justin while her mind raced, wondering about the mystery man in the costume. She felt guilty for sucking off and fucking someone else, but she couldn't do anything about it now.

Her pulse raced just thinking about how hot it'd been with Scarecrow, though. No man had ever made her scream with her climax before. Though she was texting Justin, a small part of her wondered about this Scarecrow. Kenzie chewed on her bottom lip. She knew she should be mad and maybe even scared that he'd taken advantage of her, but she wasn't. Did she know him? Was he a secret admirer? Or was he just some horny guy who saw an opportunity and took it?

Lena's beer, which was still half full, lolled to the side as her eyes closed. She'd been working so hard at the bar and finishing up her senior year. Kenzie took the beer from Lena's slack grip, and Lena stretched her long legs across the couch as she rolled over onto her side. Kenzie took the chenille throw from the end of the couch and covered her drunk roommate with it so she wouldn't wake up cold the next morning.

C. CYAN

Who are you, Scarecrow?

For the first time in months, she wasn't thinking about Justin when her head hit the pillow.

CHAPTER 7

He awoke thinking of her.

Frankenstein's bride.

Dark curtains blocked out the sunny morning, but he knew it had to be nearly midday. How many days over the past year had he turned over and slept most of the day away in a fog of depression? How many days had he laid there wondering how he would end his miserable existence?

Pills? A gunshot to the temple? Carbon monoxide? A noose? Fire?

Now, it was different. He had a purpose. Vaughn was dead, and Justin was next. A smirk played at the corner of his mouth. He swiped his palm over his scruffy face, and he smelled her perfume again. He hadn't washed her away before hitting the pillow.

For the first time in a year, it wasn't only revenge that filled his mind.

It was the curve of her soft, strong thigh, the mischievous grin on her dark red lips, the spicy perfume at her throat. Those glittering dark eyes lit up by a desire from within.

He gritted his teeth.

The way she'd said *his* name. *Justin.*

Not Travis.

He felt a small twinge of guilt for letting the woman think he was her boyfriend last night. It'd been wrong, he knew, but so much about him was wrong these days. And it'd been so long since he'd touched a woman. It had felt more exquisite than he ever remembered.

Before, when he'd been one of the guys in Greyer's entourage, it was nothing for women to throw themselves at him. He'd been just as bad as the rest of them. Sex meant nothing, and women were disposable.

Her red panties, the ones he'd cut off her last night, lay by the lamp on his bedside table. He touched the delicate lace with his index finger and thumb.

He closed his eyes and saw the glint of her eyes in the darkness again as she knelt before him and took his cock into her mouth. So trusting. Filled with desire. He'd felt powerful and alive again.

Still, he'd wanted to strangle her with his dick for saying Justin's name. For a second, he thought about pounding her so hard, she'd never say Justin's name again. Not only did he hate Justin, but he also hated the idea of Justin Greyer touching her. Her spicy scent, her soft skin, and her bouncing tits inches from his face.

His cock was rock hard. He wished he'd tasted her pussy before he fucked her. That was his only regret about last night.

He'd felt her in the most intimate way, but because he kept his mask on, he didn't get a taste. He bet she was just as spicy and sweet as she smelled.

Should he go to her again and get his fill one last time? He could drink her in and revel in her taste without her even knowing that it wasn't Justin between her legs. He wanted to so badly.

Justin had taken everything away from him when all he wanted was acceptance. Maybe it was time to take something away from Justin.

As he slid his palm over his cock, he imagined sticking his tongue into her mouth in the dark safety of the forest. And as he imagined making her scream again just by fucking her pussy with his tongue, he came in his hand.

After a shower, Travis went out to mix up the concrete to fill in the well. No one would ever find Vaughn, but he had bigger plans for Justin. He worked tirelessly mixing the concrete with water and shoveling it into the well. The afternoon sun dipped down behind the trees of the forest before his work was finished. Finally, he pulled the piece of wood back over the opening of the mouth of the well. Though he was certain the stench was gone, he swore he still smelled a whiff of it every now and then. He was drenched with sweat, and his biceps and back ached.

He'd grown accustomed to living in the shadows and the darkness, so when he went back into the mansion, he showered again without turning on the lights. Besides, it was easier to ignore the monster looking back at him in the mirror under the deceptive and forgiving cloak of gloom.

C. CYAN

As the night drew near, he didn't wonder where Justin might be. He thought only of Frankenstein's bride. If he wasn't careful, she'd ruin everything.

CHAPTER 8

Kenzie walked down the spook trail to where her bales of hay and jack-o'-lantern waited. The orange and red sky turned to a hazy purple as clouds moved in, obscuring the light from the moon. She pulled out her phone once she'd lit the candle in her pumpkin.

> You here tonight?

> Yep.

> Will you stop by and see me before we leave?

Realizing how needy she sounded, she rolled her eyes. She hated to beg for his cock, but she'd definitely beg if she had to. She still craved him, even if the mystery man had shaken her to her core the night before.

> Might have time.

Kenzie pouted. Maybe he'd already lost interest. Damn. Or maybe whoever she'd fucked the night before had told Justin about her slutty performance. She bit her lip. *Shit.* If that was it, she'd be so embarrassed.

She didn't have much time to think about it because before long, she was busy scaring each group that came down the path and having the time of her life doing it. Hours passed before she thought about Justin again.

Eventually, the spaces between groups widened out, and the night slowed. She glanced at her phone, but there were no more messages from Justin. It was almost 11.

Kenzie was sliding her phone back into her bag when she felt the knife on the back of her neck. He pressed it into her flesh, forcing her to her knees. Her breathing increased. She heard him unzip his zipper, and the sound sent waves of heat to her pussy. She shivered, but it wasn't from the cold settling into the night air.

The knife at her neck told her this wasn't Justin. Would she let this stranger fuck her again?

Imagining him pulling his enormous cock out of his pants, she licked her lips and wanted to turn to him, but the knife point kept her still. She heard him massaging his cock with his big, rough hand, and she smiled as her hand went to her clit. She hadn't worn panties tonight. Her middle finger swirled around and slid over her clit, and her breath heaved with desire. She wished his mouth was on her clit, sucking her to an orgasm.

She felt the point of the knife move from the nape of her neck, and she slowly turned. In the candlelight, the man stood there with one hand pulling back the skin of his cock, the tip purple and engorged, ready for her warm mouth. Her eyes slowly moved up. He wore all black, and tonight, he had on a demon mask. She saw the glint of his eyes beyond the crazed leer of the mask as he waited to fuck her mouth again. She wondered who he could be, and it sent a shiver of thrilling need throughout her body.

Her heart pounding in her chest, Kenzie took his cock in her hand, the weight of it solid, if not a bit intimidating. She knew from last night that she could take it, though. And she wanted all of it—and in every hole he wanted to fuck. She'd take him however he wanted her. That knowledge, that she'd let this guy—this stranger—have his way with her, made her feel slutty, but even sexier. Her body hummed with need.

Kenzie licked the tip of his cock, then swirled her tongue around the sensitive rim of his head. She heard him sigh as she took him fully into her mouth, and she smiled around his dick. He grabbed her hair, and she expected him to fuck her mouth again, but he pulled her off his dick. It came out of her mouth with a suctioned pop.

"You want to fuck a monster again?" It came out more of a growl than as words.

Kenzie nodded, biting into her bottom lip with anticipation.

He grabbed her wrist and pulled her toward the woods.

"So you want privacy tonight?" she asked as he pushed her forward while gripping her arm above the elbow. They walked only a little ways into the woods and away from the light of the jack-o'-lantern before he pushed her forward again.

"Lie down," he growled.

She liked him telling her what to do. How did he make his voice so gruff and so deep? Was it the costume? Or did desire do that to his voice? She should have known last night that this wasn't Justin. Justin's voice was smooth and not nearly as deep. This man's voice was gruff and scratchy. She couldn't even tell his age.

Kenzie glanced at the leaf-strewn ground. "Wouldn't you rather go back to my place?" she asked as she obeyed him. The ground was cold and wet from the dew that had fallen already. Even now, a fog swirled around them, and she felt chilled.

"Shut up," he said.

As much as she wanted to be fucked again tonight, this wasn't as fun as it'd been last night. Maybe it was the demon mask. It made him look more sinister than the scarecrow, which had only been creepy. Chill bumps rose on her arms, and she wasn't sure if it was from the cold or from fear. He looked fucking scary tonight. Besides, this guy could be anyone. Terror tugged at her, willing her to get up and run, but her own dark needs pulled at the deepest part of her core, and despite her trepidation, she trembled with desire for the masked man. Whoever he was.

The demon knelt between her legs and spread her knees apart. He laid down the knife and slid both hands up her thighs, pushing up her skirt as he went. His eyes glittered beyond the mask as he watched her. Warmth flooded her core again, and she laid back on her elbows, ready for whatever he had in store for her.

When he saw she wasn't wearing panties this time, he laughed a deep, rumbling sound that made her simultaneously want to crawl away from him and also shove her pussy into his face. She didn't have to do anything, though, because he grasped her ass cheeks and pulled her to him so that she fell flat on her back.

Kenzie looked down and gasped. He must have pulled up the mask because she saw its evil visage still leering at her as if a demon was analyzing her, like a two-headed fiend lapping at her sopping pussy. His tongue plunged into her hole, and she writhed as he licked at her clit, then fucked her with his tongue, back and forth between teasing her clit and tongue-fucking her. He was masterful at it.

The demon knelt before her in the most reverent worship. Whoever this was lapped her up like the most exquisite thing he'd ever put into his mouth. The masked man wanted her to orgasm. He insisted on it with every flick of the tongue. It wasn't like last night when he took what he wanted, whether she liked it or not (though she'd loved it). Tonight seemed to be about her.

Kenzie leaned her head back, feeling weightless and euphoric as she enjoyed the wonderful tongue assault. She looked at the trees looming over them until she couldn't keep her eyes open any longer. She felt the pleasure rising to a peak until she grabbed his hair and mask, squirming in ecstasy. He didn't let up sucking at her swollen clit, and she dug the heels of her boots into the moist earth and writhed under his hands. His fingers dug into her hips as she rode out her orgasm. As wave after wave hit her, she squeezed his head between her knees and bucked against his face.

When her eyes fluttered back open, she saw him rising from between her legs, but it was too dark to see his face. The mask had fallen off, but he grabbed it and pulled it back on quickly. He still wanted to role-play, it seemed.

The game continues, then. Kenzie smirked. He still thought she believed he was Justin.

Before she could get her bearings, he pulled her legs onto his shoulders and pushed deep inside her soaked pussy. His cock met little resistance because she was so sloppy and wet. She was swollen from her orgasm, and though there was little resistance, he felt too large for her at the moment. She winced at the bittersweet feeling. He took big, long strokes as he pulled her bustier down to reveal her breasts, which bounced every time he pushed back into her.

As she bounced, the demon face blurred into a frenzied glare. *Maybe he is a demon*, she thought in a daze. He stilled for a moment, and the demon's face floated just above hers as he whispered, "I'm going to make you scream for me again, one way or another."

It sounded like a warning, one that she should be terrified of, but she grabbed his shoulders and used her legs to roll him over so that she was on top of him. She'd never had two orgasms almost simultaneously before, but if anyone could do it for her, this man would.

Still wearing the mask, the stranger underneath her held her waist as she rode his cock up and down, her titties bouncing near his face. She imagined the demon licking her nipples with a long black tongue, biting each one that got too close to his sharp teeth. Fuck, it was hot screwing a guy in a mask. She already felt the energy building for another one, and as much as she wanted it, she wanted to stay in this moment for as long as she could.

"Kiss me," she murmured. She wanted his mouth on her, and she wanted to look at him.

"No."

She frowned down at the demon.

"I can't hear you scream if my tongue is in your mouth."

He rose to meet her, to plunge and grind against her until the energy unwound itself, to unfurl within her like a sinister pulsation. He reached up with one big hand and grabbed her hair, pulling her head back. Like an exorcism, the pent-up energy released from her body, making her eyes roll back in her head and her toes curl. The sound she released was half guttural howl and half squeal of delight. An onlooker might have thought that this was an actual exorcism.

"Good girl," he whispered as he thrust into her melting body. With a grunt, he pumped his seed into her hot, throbbing pussy as he slipped his fingers down the crack of her ass and pushed against her asshole. "If I had it in me, that'd be mine tonight, too."

He slipped out of her, and she slid to her side on the ground next to him, her chest heaving from the exertion.

What was it about the bad guys? She'd always found them so appealing, but it never turned out very well. It was part of the reason she'd found Justin enticing. He was one of those proper rich guys with values and etiquette. So different from the boys she dated in high school. She was looking for someone special when she met him.

And yet, here she was on her back for some guy dressed as a demon. And she found it incredibly hot. What the hell was wrong with her?

Kenzie didn't want to break the spell this sexy, virile man had somehow cast over her, but she needed to know. "Who the hell are you?"

CHAPTER 9

In high school, Justin Reese Greyer was the big man on campus. His dad owned Greyer Aerospace, an aircraft manufacturing company with over $8 billion in annual revenue that employed over 15,000 people. On top of that, his grandfather had been governor before Justin was born and had since bought up a large amount of farmland in the state and in two neighboring states.

Justin's father and Travis' dad had grown up together, so the two boys were always thrown together when the families attended the same events. In high school, Justin allowed Travis to be a part of the group. Most of the guys liked Travis better, and Justin knew it. There was always an unspoken resentment between them. Travis was never totally at ease around him. Because he was younger and because his family was wealthy but not filthy rich, the pecking order dictated that Travis stay in the shadows of Justin's limelight, at least until he graduated.

Women had been disposable to Justin. And for a time, Travis felt the same way. Girls threw themselves at all of them, and Travis gave no thought to monogamy or to treating women decently. None of them did.

"Females are meant to be banged and sent on their way," Justin often said.

It was a hollow way to live, Travis came to realize. He'd met a girl that he liked for more than her body. Her mind and her artistry intrigued him. Bee, short for Beatrice, loved dark poetry and music. She made charcoal drawings that amazed him. Travis never claimed her as his girlfriend, but their relationship morphed naturally into spending most days together.

During Justin's senior year of high school, which was Travis' junior year, the buried animosity between the two came to a head at a party. The guys chided him for being such a homebody lately, so Travis went with them to the party of the week at someone's house that he didn't even know. It was a beautiful three-story modern home on a lake, and it was lit up and full of people. Cars lined the street leading up to it. Loud music thumped from speakers somewhere in the house.

When they finally made it inside, the crowd parted as if it had been waiting for Travis' entrance. Then, he saw it. There, on the couch, was Justin with Beatrice's head in his lap, drooling from whatever drug he'd given her. Her skirt was hiked up so that he saw the red marks across her thigh from someone grabbing her forcefully. Justin had his hand in her shirt, fondling her breast.

"Ah, the golden boy is here. Come join us, friend."

"Get your hands off Bee," Travis said as he strode toward them and towered over Justin, his fists clenched at his sides. "You bastard."

Justin's eyebrows drew together with mock concern. "She begged for my cock, man. So I let her have it."

Travis tried to keep his voice steady and his seething anger under control. "You drugged her."

"Nope, she was already fucked up when I got here. Somebody said she sucked off the host in the bathroom for some coke. You sure know how to pick 'em, man." He shoved her off his lap and stood. "Really, you dodged a bullet with this hoe. Better off without her."

When Justin turned to look down at Bee, unconscious on the couch, Travis punched him in the neck. He went down, but not for long. Justin was on a cocaine high, Travis realized, when the motherfucker sprang back up like a jack-in-the-box. Physically, Justin was smaller than Travis, but the stimulant had given him a temporary advantage. He punched at Travis like a Rock'em Sock'em Robot—four punches before Travis knew what was happening. Travis had the strength, though, and one more punch landed right on Justin's temple, and he went down again. This time, he didn't get up so fast, and Travis got a kick at his ribs before the other guys pulled him off Justin.

The rest of the semester, which was only about eight more weeks of school, the guys didn't have much to do with Travis, at least while Justin was around. Travis and Justin kept things civil, but the gulf between them widened.

Travis and Bee never recovered what they had before that night. She admitted that she had taken drugs before going to the party, and he couldn't trust her anymore.

Travis was relieved when Justin graduated and went off to college.

It wouldn't be the end of it, though.

CHAPTER 10

"Who are you?" Kenzie repeated.

"I'm just a man with time to kill." Travis knew she wouldn't catch his double-meaning, but he laughed at his pun. He actually *didn't* have time. He scrambled up. It was getting late, and he needed to find Justin before they closed up the haunted attraction for good. He looked over his shoulder as he zipped his pants. She was stuffing her breasts back into her bustier. "How did you know I wasn't Justin, anyway?" A part of him suspected she knew he wasn't her fratboy fuck toy. And there was a tiny bit of him pleased that she'd wanted him again, knowing he wasn't Justin, as if she was choosing him.

She stood and straightened her skirt. She shook her head. "You were just fine with letting me believe I was fucking Justin."

Travis turned to her again and picked up his knife.

"You can't have that out here, you know," she said. The pitch of her voice was higher, and it made him smile behind his mask.

"I'm not an employee."

Her eyes flickered from the knife and back to his mask. "How could you do that to me? Pretend to be him and just fuck me like that without my consent."

"Oh, you were consenting," he growled. "You consented more than any woman I've ever had, in fact."

Her eyes shot up to his mask, but the hint of a smile played at her red lips. "You knew I thought you were Justin." Her words had little conviction and sounded hollow.

"Did you really?" Travis narrowed his eyes. "So you're surrounded by people in costumes, and without so much as a 'how ya doing,' you're on your knees sucking cock. He must have some kind of spell over you."

Kenzie fumed. "Justin said he, he, *argh*," she said, exasperated. "Shut up! I *did* think you were Justin. I even called you by his name."

"Could you not tell I'm bigger than Justin or that my dick wasn't his? I've seen his dick, and it doesn't compare." He smirked behind his mask.

"I wouldn't know. I've never seen his dick." Kenzie crossed her arms over her chest.

Shocked by her admission, he paused. He'd assumed Justin had already been all over her. He could tell that she wasn't surprised when he'd revealed he wasn't Justin, though. She could try to bullshit him, and maybe herself, too, all she wanted. "The fantasy was Justin, but you really didn't care that it wasn't him. Admit it. Deep down, you knew the scarecrow wasn't Justin, and you still wanted it."

Travis saw Kenzie falter. She frowned.

"Look, I don't have time for this. Go on with your job, and let me get to mine."

"You said you didn't work here," she pointed out.

"I don't."

"Then, what are you doing?" she asked. Her eyes glanced back at the knife at his side.

He stepped toward her so that she could see his eyes. "If I told you, I'd have to kill you." There was no humor in his tone. He'd hoped that would give her enough pause to let him go, but to his surprise, she laughed. It was a deep, throaty laugh. It made his dick twitch again, thinking about how he had it down her throat the night before. This woman was distracting him.

Travis turned and walked away.

"Where are you going?" she called after him.

He heard her following by the crunch of the leaves under her boots.

"To find Justin."

"Why?"

Travis glanced back at her. "I'm gonna kill the bastard."

She gave him a surprised look that turned stern as the space between her eyebrows narrowed and pulled down in the center. "What? No, wait." She ran forward and grabbed his arm.

"Are you insane, woman? A guy has a knife—you don't go grabbing him. You're defenseless, and that's a good way to get killed."

She pursed her lips together. "You aren't going to kill me." She gulped, and her eyes searched his. "If you were going to, you already would have," she said, just above a whisper.

Travis gritted his teeth against the frustration this woman was causing him. "I'll cut your big tits off and shove them down your fucking throat so you choke on them. How about that?"

Her eyes widened, and she turned her head like a dog does when it's perplexed. "Who are you?" She moved to grab his mask, and he slapped her hand away. "Ouch."

"Touch me again, and you're dead," Travis said through clenched teeth.

She narrowed her eyes. "Fine, psycho. Go on a killing spree. Lotta good that'll do."

This woman had some nerve. "You don't know anything," he said, walking away from her. His voice came out low, filled with more resignation than he'd realized he was feeling at the moment.

"So tell me why, then. Help me understand."

Travis stopped. Nothing he could say would make her understand the vileness of the guy she thought she knew. "Stay away from him. If I don't get to him first, leave him alone. You deserve better. I can feel that in my bones, and I don't even know your name." He gripped the knife tighter in his hand and walked toward where he thought he'd finally sink it into Justin's guts, a sense of purpose propelling him toward his fate.

"Kenzie," she called out. "Who are you?"

He kept walking. Then, she said the one thing that could make him stop in his tracks.

"Serves me right for beginning to fall for a monster."

She'd muttered it to herself, but he heard her.

Travis stopped, turned, and strode toward her so fast that she took a couple of steps backward in surprise. The fear came off her in waves as he leaned down so that the nose of the demon mask touched her cheek. "You have no fucking idea what kind of monster I am." He was trembling from trying to restrain his anger, and he gripped her arm with his free hand. "Get the fuck away from me."

She trembled under his gaze as tears rimmed her eyes. When he pushed her away, she fled. He thought he'd never forget the image of her skirt flying out in waves behind her. His beautiful Bride of Frankenstein. Scaring her away was the only way he knew how to save her from the chaos that had become his existence, from the chaos that would consume him.

Before the week was over, he expected to be dead, and she was better off not wasting her time with him.

CHAPTER 11

Kenzie paused on the path to catch her breath. She swallowed the lump in her throat and willed her pounding heart to slow down. What was with this damn guy?

Kenzie touched her face where he'd pressed his mask into her cheek. What was with *her*? Why was she even considering turning around? He was obviously completely off his fucking rocker.

Yet, she was torn.

There was something in his voice, in the way he'd nearly begged her to stay away from Justin, that made her pause. Would a cold-blooded killer even care if Justin might somehow hurt her?

Yet, his words rang true. *You have no fucking idea what kind of monster I am.* She believed every syllable.

And what about Justin? Should she give him a heads-up? This guy had a knife, and he seemed pretty dead-set on going after Justin. Was he really going to kill Justin? Kenzie believed the demon intended to, and it was her duty as Justin's friend to at least warn him.

She pulled out her phone, unlocked it, and hovered her thumb over the messages. What exactly was she going to tell Justin? She'd met some delusional guy with a mask—a man she'd screwed who revealed that he was out to get Justin? She didn't even know a name to tell him.

Kenzie frowned as darkness roiled in her stomach. What had Justin done to piss off the guy in the mask? Or was the guy just deranged? She looked back toward where the masked demon had disappeared into the darkness. Why was she hesitating?

> Where are you?

She noticed her hands were trembling. *Answer, dammit.* Now was not the time to ignore her. "C'mon, Justin," she whispered.

Several seconds ticked by as she headed down the trail where she thought Justin might be. It was darker than normal, with clouds covering the moon, and she tripped over a tree root but recovered before hitting the ground. Her phone tumbled from her hand. She bent to pick it up as a crack of thunder rumbled in the distance. Thunder meant the Spook Trail was shutting down. Mr. Jameson wouldn't allow people out here if a storm was coming.

Kenzie's phone vibrated with a new message.

> Heading toward the front. A storm is coming.

Lights along the trail came on to alert patrons that Jameson's Haunted Farm was closing early for the night. She sighed in relief. The wind had picked up, and the lights swayed, casting a rocking glow and creating deep, moving shadows that made the skin on her arms prickle. She smoothed her hand over one arm and looked back to her station on the trail.

She stopped to blow out the candle in her jack-o'-lantern, and she slung her bag over her shoulder. If Justin was heading toward the front where all the people were, he was safe. For now. Hopefully. She'd need to warn him, though.

Kenzie didn't think about that for long because she saw the guy with the knife coming back toward her. She quickly hid when he rounded the curve in the trail. He'd assume she was long gone. She still couldn't see him for the demon mask, but she could tell by the tension in his shoulders and in his gait that he was pissed at this turn of events. Another rumble of thunder sounded as he took off through the trees, away from the trail.

Kenzie had to know what this was about. And right now, this was the only opportunity she might ever have to follow him and find out where he was going, who he was, and why he wanted her crush dead.

Was that the only reason she wanted to follow him? She wasn't sure. But she felt an intense pull to him, and she trusted her instincts, despite the fear that almost overwhelmed her.

The demon disappeared into the thicket. She waited a few more seconds to allow him to get ahead of her, and then, she followed him into the dark forest.

CHAPTER 12

F^{*uck*}.

The blood pounded in Travis' ears so hard from his seething anger, he was practically deaf from it.

How could one bastard be so lucky? It was as if Fate put Justin up on a pedestal all by himself for the world to fall at his feet and worship him. His plan had completely backfired, and all because Travis couldn't keep his dick in his pants. That fucking girl had ruined it, and he might never get a chance to kill Justin and exact the revenge he'd been planning for months.

No, there was no going back. Travis wouldn't let that bastard live. He'd just have to get into the car and find the motherfucker tonight. It *had* to be tonight.

Travis had been stomping so hard through the fall foliage and swatting limbs and vines out of his face with such vehemence that he didn't realize he'd gotten to the old well already.

He stopped when he saw it, the pale outline in the darkness. The clouds covered the moon, and a rumble of thunder promised the storm would be here soon, but he knew the well, even in the inky darkness. Cicadas and crickets hummed low. The wind rattled dead leaves in the trees overhead. A bolt of lightning lit up the night, and the well glowed for a moment like a lonely beacon.

Travis sighed, the anger unfurling his tense muscles and beginning to dissipate.

It wasn't her fault. Kenzie.

Kenzie.

Frenzy.

That's just what she'd put him into.

A fucking frenzy. Literally.

He would have laughed, but he felt like crying. He pulled the mask from his face. It was hot and made breathing difficult. He crushed the demon's visage in his fist.

Kenzie didn't do this on purpose. Until he'd opened his stupid fucking mouth, she hadn't even known what he was headed to do. Why did he care if she was another one of Justin's casualties? By now, she'd surely given Justin the head's up, and Justin would be waiting for him.

Fuck!

He wanted to rage, but that wouldn't do him any good.

Barreling through the forest like a damned monster wouldn't either.

He needed to get his head back on straight.

"Traviiiissss," a voice hissed.

Travis' eyes snapped toward the well. His heart must have completely stopped, along with his breathing.

Was it the wind in the trees? Was he losing his fucking mind? He'd lost everything else. Why not?

"Traviiiissss." It was more like a hiss than a whisper. He took a step toward it.

"I know you're there." The sound of a man's voice from deep inside the well, barely audible above the wind, reached his ears.

He knew that voice well.

Vaughn.

Except that wasn't possible. No one was down there. Alive anyway. The four bags of cement he'd poured over Vaughn's body had assured him of that, even if the smell of decaying flesh hadn't been enough assurance.

Travis broke out into a cold sweat. He stared at the well. Was he cracking up?

"Traviiiissss."

Travis took a few more tentative steps toward the well. "Shut the fuck up." His voice boomed in the forest's silence. It had much more bravado to it than he actually felt at the moment. His hands trembled, and he clenched them into fists. Even the insects ceased their incessant hum at the sound of his words. Travis fought the overwhelming urge to flee. His senses were now alert, almost superhumanly sensitive. Another rumble of thunder sounded, and he could smell the rain coming. Then, the snap of a twig.

His already hammering heart nearly leaped out of his chest. Travis gripped the knife in his fist and clenched his jaw, ready to fight. He turned his head slowly, half-expecting to see Justin behind him.

Or maybe Vaughn's ghost. He wasn't sure.

Who he hadn't expected to see was Kenzie.

His hammering heart dropped into his stomach.

As if on cue, a bolt of lightning streaked the sky and lit up the dark woods.

Terror crossed Kenzie's pretty features, and she opened her mouth to scream as she glimpsed his scarred face.

Travis' heart broke all over again.

CHAPTER 13

The fight at the house party the night Bee betrayed him wasn't the last Travis would see of Justin, but for a while, Travis was free of him. While Justin went off to college, Travis spent his senior year at the top of his game. With Justin gone, he was the most popular guy on campus. He dated a few girls, but his failed relationship with Bee had changed him. He could no longer treat them like trash, as he had before Bee, but he also didn't trust them. Maybe he'd never trust a woman to be faithful again. It'd left a roiling ache in his stomach that wouldn't subside. Was there such a thing as relationship PTSD? If so, he had it. And it kept him from getting close to anyone he dated. So he kept them at arm's length and dropped them when things got serious.

To add to his misery, Travis lost both parents near the end of his senior year. He was suddenly the man of the house, the gargantuan mansion in the hills of Tennessee, and he was utterly alone. It's a miracle he even finished his senior year and graduated. If not for a coach who'd taken it upon himself to make sure Travis graduated, he'd have never walked across that stage.

Not knowing what else to do with himself, Travis enrolled in the college that had accepted him before the car accident that killed his parents. When they'd discussed his plans after high school, his dad insisted he pledge some fraternities, though he said he didn't care which fraternity Travis ended up in. Travis knew that his dad really wanted him to be a part of the one he was in years ago. How could Travis ignore the last thing his father had wanted for him?

So Travis trudged up the steps of the three-story brick mansion and immaculate landscaping lit up with obnoxiously bright spotlights along with the other guys pledging the illustrious frat that night, and he'd found himself face to face with Justin Reese Greyer, III, again.

To Travis' surprise, Justin acted as though nothing had happened between them, like they were even long-lost friends. Justin gave him that same wide grin he'd greeted Travis with for most of his life. Justin clapped him on the back after shaking his hand and introduced Travis to his frat brothers. Maybe this was a fresh start for them.

"This is one helluva guy. I've known him practically all my life. Our house would be lucky to have him," Justin said, his speech a bit slurred from drinking. He tipped back a red cup of something and led Travis throughout the house, introducing him to all the guys he'd soon call his own fraternity brothers. Vaughn, Freddy, Caleb, and others, the most important and affluent men on campus.

Travis was a bit baffled by the warm welcome from Justin, but he wouldn't look a gift horse in the mouth. Travis' father's wish was more important to him than just about anything else. Even if Justin hadn't welcomed him, Travis would have pledged.

Of course, there was the matter of hazing that comes with joining a frat. Hazing doesn't happen at any of these colleges, of course, *wink, wink.*

The night of their initiation, they loaded up the pledges into the back of pickup trucks and SUVs. The frat brothers blindfolded the pledges and took them out into the country before hauling them out of the vehicles roughly. One by one, they tied each pledge's hands behind his back and led him to the end of a pier.

Travis could tell this by the feel and creak of the boards underfoot and the smell of the water in the night breeze. They weren't bluffing about where they were when they told each pledge that he was going to walk off the end of the pier with his hands still tied to prove his dedication and trust in the fraternity. Travis just hoped there were frat brothers in the water ready to catch him.

After reciting somber vows, each man took a step forward, sure he was about to plunge into the chilly water and possibly drown, only to feel more pier beneath his feet. When Travis stepped forward and found the solid boards underfoot, he huffed a sigh of relief. Justin pulled off Travis' blindfold, chuckled, and clapped him on the shoulder before untying his hands.

"Welcome to the brotherhood." Justin wasn't smiling. There was a strange light in his eyes, almost a taunting look. Or maybe Travis was imagining things in the dark.

"Thanks," he mumbled. Travis tried to shake his apprehension of Justin. To be fraternity brothers, they needed to bury the past behind them. Travis would have to learn to trust Justin again.

They headed back to the field where the rest of the brothers stood around a raging bonfire, drinking and listening to country music from one of the pickup trucks. Travis drank a few beers but didn't want to get shitfaced. He still wasn't sure if this was all that the guys had in store for them tonight, and because he didn't know these guys that well, he wanted to be as self-aware as possible. It seemed light for hazing. Had they gotten off that lucky?

Every time Travis refused a beer, though, someone would look at him as if he was committing a social faux pas by passing on the booze. "Drink up," they demanded, and he gave in to the peer pressure.

Travis took his time but still had eight or ten beers in him when the guys were all loaded back up in the vehicles to head back to the frat house for more partying. His vision was swimmy, but he wasn't too drunk. Travis tried to get into an SUV so he'd be less jostled around, but Justin grabbed his arm and pushed him toward his own truck. "Get in," Justin said. "You're my responsibility tonight, ol' buddy, ol' pal."

Travis didn't like his tone of voice, and he frowned before climbing into the back and sitting down with his back to the cab. A few other new recruits climbed in, and soon, they were flying down gravel roads, the dust blinding and choking him.

Either the road was ridiculously curvy, or Justin was trying to make them all vomit by swerving left and right. Travis wagered it was the latter.

At one point, a black guy named Keith almost flipped over the side of the truck. He would have if Travis hadn't grabbed his shirt and pulled him back into the bed of the truck. "Whoa!" he said. Keith's eyes were wide as he slid lower to make sure he didn't fall out. He laughed nervously as Travis shook his head. It was enough to sober Travis up a good bit.

Travis saw the headlights of Vaughn's SUV directly behind them. Justin slammed on the brakes, which pitched Travis forward. He hit his head against the bed of the truck, and he felt a trickle of warm blood as black spots dotted his vision. "Ow! Son of a bitch!" The last thing he needed was a concussion a few weeks into his first semester of college.

Dust swirled around them like a thick, tan fog as he stood up in the back of the truck, annoyed with Justin's antics. Justin was going to injure someone if he didn't stop. Travis tapped on the back glass of the cab to tell Justin to cut the bullshit out when Justin punched the gas again. Travis lost his balance and tumbled over the side of the truck.

Not seeing him in the dust from the gravel road, Vaughn, in the SUV behind them, followed Justin's lead and lurched forward. Travis felt the excruciating impact of the wheels bouncing over his body and the undercarriage snatching at his flesh, dragging him.

Then, everything went black.

CHAPTER 14

"What the fuck did you do?" It was Justin's voice, but it sounded warped and far away.

"Ah, fuck, I've been drinking. My dad's a politician. They'll crucify me for this." That was Vaughn's voice, but he sounded like he was at the bottom of a barrel. And he sounded like he was crying.

"Calm down," Travis heard who he thought was Caleb talking to Vaughn.

Justin said, "Hey, y'all stay in the fucking truck and mind your business."

Help. Travis blinked, but he couldn't move. Not even his mouth would open. He was having trouble breathing. It came out in ragged huffs, and he couldn't get enough air to fill his lungs.

The cold stars swirled above him. He thought he might pass out again, and he willed the swimming stars to still.

Help.

He thought the word, willing them to hear it, but it would never escape his lips.

Why weren't they trying to help him? Why weren't they checking on him or calling an ambulance? He tried to clear the pounding in his head, pressing his eyes closed again. He needed help, but he couldn't speak to plead with them for it. *Maybe help is already on the way,* he thought as he smelled the metallic scent of his own blood. He was aware of tall grass nearby and several people shuffling around him, but he couldn't call out to them, as he couldn't get enough breath to make a sound. It took all his energy just to breathe in and out in shallow little wheezes.

"What are we gonna do?" This was a voice Travis didn't recognize.

After a pause, he heard Justin's voice again, low, and with a tone of finality. "Leave him."

Had Travis heard right? Was Justin, who'd known Travis his entire life, going to leave him for dead on the side of the road?

"What?" Vaughn asked.

"He separated from the group and ran off," Justin continued. "None of us saw him after the bonfire. We assumed he hitchhiked back to town. Got it?"

There were a few murmurs before the guys, his so-called *brothers*, got back into their vehicles and left Travis for dead.

***

Travis didn't die, though there were many days ahead in which he wished he had. His body lived on, but a human part of him died that night on that gravel road.

He didn't know how he'd been found or how he ended up in a hospital, but weeks later, he woke up in Nashville. When he came out of the medically induced coma, he remembered his parents were dead, and he found himself utterly alone. He remembered graduating from high school and starting college. Then, a flood of memories from that night washed over him, the hazing, the truck ride, and finally lying on the side of the road dying. He cried like a baby as nurses tried to calm him.

While people far worthier than he–children, young lovers, fathers and mothers, teachers, and firefighters–died every day, he was doomed to continue to live an excruciating and wretched life barely worth living. If he tried to ignore the gashes and eventual scars, the pain and aching tenderness of his wounds were a constant reminder of what he'd gone through.

A detective came to talk to him about that night, but he refused to answer the man's questions. Travis didn't want to relive the trauma and cry like a baby in front of this stranger, even if it would have gotten the frat brothers in trouble. He knew how things worked. Justin and the rest of them had plenty of money. They wouldn't get much more than a slap on the wrist for what they'd done if Travis told on them.

The doctors performed surgery after surgery, grafting skin, screwing bones back into place, and trying to make him look like a semblance of the man he'd once been. Even the best plastic surgeons in the area couldn't completely fix him. An ugly scar ran along the right side of his face, down his temple and jaw, and every time he looked in the mirror, he saw Justin's treachery. Justin, Vaughn, and the others had made him into a monster of a man pieced together—and barely alive.

Another terrible scar ran down his right hip and thigh, and the doctors worked on his femoral shaft fracture twice before leaving him to heal. He had to learn to walk again. A grown man wobbling around like a baby was a new level of frustrating embarrassment. He welcomed the pain of each session because it meant that he was getting stronger. He rode the pain like a chariot into war in this battle that was just beginning.

Travis walked faster than they anticipated, and he returned to the mansion within eight months. He hit the gym in his basement to strengthen his other muscles, too, and before long, he was strong again.

Stronger.

Because now, Travis had a kind of fortitude that he could never have had in his old life. And he had a purpose.

He'd make them pay.

CHAPTER 15

The way the light hit him, the way it tunneled into the gash along his jaw, made it appear deeper. With the anger flashing in his eyes with every strike of lightning, it gave her masked man a look even more sinister than the demon mask had, and she'd gasped. She saw in his pained expression how horrible that reaction was from her, how it had cut into him, and she wished she could take it back.

"You frightened me. That's all," Kenzie said.

"I tend to do that to people," he murmured as he turned his scars away from her.

"No, I didn't realize you'd stopped. You've made me jumpy tonight with the stuff about Justin, and I needed—" He brought the demon mask up as if to put it back on, but she held out her hand to stop him. "Don't."

He cut his eyes toward her but still didn't turn to fully face her. "Why are you following me?"

Kenzie ignored his question. "Who were you talking to?"

"Go back to the spook trail, Kenzie. Forget you ever met me." His voice was deep and gravelly and filled with sadness. He turned, walking away.

"No." Kenzie followed, despite the fast pace he was moving in front of her. This man, this sad, broken man who made her feel things she'd never felt before, couldn't just walk into the night and away from her forever.

When she stumbled over a dead limb, he stopped and swore.

"I'm fine," she said as she pulled herself up. She heard the rain before it hit her skin. Cold, fat droplets splattered against her head and arms, and before she knew it, the rain was coming down in torrents. There was nowhere to go to get out of the storm.

"No, you're infuriating is what you are." Lightning streaked the sky just left of them, and he ducked instinctively. He grabbed her hand, and they ran. He pulled her along as the underbrush tore at her skirt and as the rain soaked through her dress. As they ran, she realized just how massive he was across the shoulders. How had she ever mistaken this guy for Justin?

She didn't know where they were headed, but it had to be better than out in the middle of a thunderstorm. Within ten minutes, she was tiring from the water weighing her dress down—and from trying to keep herself upright while running across the slippery, wet woods. Finally, she saw the hulking form of a barn appear out of the gloom of the pouring rain. They ran inside, and he pushed the door shut against the wind and the slanted curtains of rain.

Kenzie was drenched. Her Frankenstein's bride's updo had fallen to wet curls at her shoulders, and she could just imagine what the makeup looked like from all the water on her face. She was probably more ghoulish than the demon mask at this point. Her chest heaved as she tried to catch her breath, and she caught his eyes on the shadows at her cleavage, which only made her nipples pebble more. Her teeth chattered. She wasn't sure if it was from the cold or from being here with him. It wasn't fear she felt, but... anticipation.

The barn smelled of hay, dust, and motor oil. She could make out the form of a car covered by a cloth. He strode over to it and pulled it away to reveal a shiny blue 1972 Lamborghini Miura.

Her eyes widened, and her mouth fell open. "Holy shit!" Kenzie pointed at the car. "Do you know what that is?" She ran over to it to touch the smooth paint. Growing up around her dad, she watched lots of car shows on TV, and he'd even dragged her to classic car shows every chance he could get. As a result, she'd learned a lot about classic cars and had grown to love them. This car was worth millions, and it was sitting in a damp old barn in the middle of nowhere.

"Yeah, it was my dad's. I can't bring myself to part with it," he said quietly.

He wrapped the cloth around her shoulders. She noticed that even this close, he tried to turn his face so that she wouldn't see his scar. Thunder rumbled outside, and the rain didn't let up.

Kenzie stepped toward him and touched the underside of his chin so that he had to look directly at her. "We'll stay warmer together." She pulled the cloth up over his shoulders so that it covered them both, leaving her hands on his shoulders. She felt the heat radiating off his skin through his wet shirt.

He groaned as he stepped closer to her, a rumble deep in his chest that made her ache. "We'll stay warmer if we're out of these wet clothes."

She leaned in so that her lips were an inch from his ear. "Are you trying to get me naked?"

Kenzie felt his lips brush her neck. "Is it working?" he asked. He pressed his lips against her cold skin. "Again?" He smiled against her neck.

She pulled back to look at him. "I still don't even know your name." She saw the green of his eyes despite the darkness of the barn. Green like the dark, dangerous forest.

He hesitated for a beat, and Kenzie thought he might not tell her.

He gave a sigh. "Travis."

CHAPTER 16

Travis was drowning. His life had changed in an instant that night on that dirt road, and now, it was rearranging and tilting him upside down again. When he'd come out of the coma and realized what he'd been through, he'd assumed his life was over. As he looked in the mirror each morning, as he looked at the pieced-together monster that Justin Reese had made him into, he had to find reasons to keep going. He'd resigned himself to revenge. It was his one and only motivation to get through the tough days ahead.

Now, though... now, there was her. He'd tried to push himself up, out of her intoxicating pull after that first night with her, but he couldn't. He knew he needed to break the surface of the exquisite hold she had on him, but he realized that he just didn't want to.

How much would he have to lose before he gave up on life altogether?

Travis pulled Kenzie close. The heat coming off her was deliciously intense. They lay in the hay naked and wrapped in the drop cloth. The sweet smell of hay that mixed with the smell of her hair was heady. He breathed in deeply. He never wanted to forget that smell.

His thumb rubbed at a smudge of black makeup at her temple. Her stitches and scars were painted on; his were all too real.

Her fingertips explored his body. They paused over his scars but then continued, leaving a trail of warmth against his skin. It was as if she were mapping his muscles and contours and wounds, learning all his valleys and peaks and imperfections. He was hard just being touched by her fingertips, but he didn't ravish her as he had earlier. He allowed her time to feel him.

A new ribbon of hope wrapped itself around him every time he was with her. Could there be more to this life than the anguish he'd suffered? He'd assumed anyone who looked at him would be disgusted, but she wasn't. Even after he took advantage of her, he didn't revolt her. He was a monster, but she didn't care about that. She saw him like no one else could.

"I'm sorry."

Kenzie looked up at him. "For what?"

"That first night on the trail. What I did... wasn't—"

"Shhh," she interrupted, and he was grateful. He was damn bad at apologies. "Some part of me knew," she whispered and pressed her lips to his chest.

She didn't want to elaborate, either, and he was fine with that. He understood that sometimes people did things in the heat of the moment that weren't rational. Sometimes, people made poor decisions, and those decisions turned things around for the better. Not every mistake had to be the end of the world. And Kenzie's mistake had been his all-time favorite.

Travis found it hard to swallow the lump forming in his throat. He remained silent so that the emotion in his voice didn't betray the tumult of emotion happening inside him. He was glad she couldn't see the tears rimming his eyes.

Before, he'd lost his will to go back to school, to find work, and even to live for a while. The only thing that had brought him back from that was hatred, but what would be the resolution of that hatred?

Death.

He'd known that for a while, and he'd been okay with that.

Now, though, he wondered what could be the resolution of love. That's what gave him pause. It made his heart pound harder as if it wanted to show him how a heart can live on and even thrive after such sadness and suffering.

If he didn't continue with his revenge against those who'd left him for dead, what kind of life could he have?

If he failed to bring Justin to justice, if he died trying, what would become of Kenzie? He could certainly never leave her in the hands of a person like Justin Reese Greyer. With Justin alive, Travis believed he would never find peace for himself. But if Travis killed Justin, there was no future with Kenzie, either.

So maybe all they had left was this one night. And if that were so, he'd relish every inch of her body.

Travis' eyes fell to her lips in the dark, which were still stained dark red from her spook trail makeup. He touched her bottom lip with his thumb. He realized that with everything they'd done together already, he hadn't kissed her. Would she want to kiss him?

Kenzie took his hand and nuzzled her cheek and mouth into his palm like a kitten might do. She ran her fingertips along the scars on his face, and he held his breath. "Does it still hurt?"

"Not so much."

"So it's okay if I touch you?" she asked.

Warmth flooded through him, knowing that she wanted to touch even the ugliest parts of him. "I want you to touch me all over."

Kenzie mounted him, pushing his hard cock down onto his stomach as she sat atop him. The heat from her pussy felt maddeningly good against his shaft, but he denied himself from impaling her with it until she was ready for it. She leaned down, the nipples of her breasts teasing the skin of his chest, and placed her hands on either side of his head. Ever so gently, cupping his damaged face in her palm, she kissed his lips. She teased his mouth with her tongue until he couldn't take it any longer and dove into her mouth, seeking every hot inch of her. He ground his dick into the channel of her pussy, and she slid back and forth against the shaft. It felt like the head of his dick would explode, and he gasped as he held himself off. His mind was a muddled mess as sensations overwhelmed him. She was so slick and hot against him that it made his toes curl. He dug his fingers into her hips as she slid her clit against his cock. Every time it hit the tip of his dick, he thought he might scream in pleasure.

"Let yourself go. I'm not going anywhere tonight," she whispered.

His balls tightened. "Ah, fuck," Travis said as he let the orgasm wash over him. He felt hot cum hit his stomach.

"I need you in me," she murmured as she rose and guided his sensitive tip in. It was almost too much for him to bear. She entwined her legs with his and drove him in deeper, her own need too strong to take it any slower. Yet, she moved against him slowly, so perfectly and so intensely slow. From the look on her face, he could tell that she was savoring the friction of their bodies, and she threw her head back as her pussy squeezed around him and released over and over until she was panting and bucking on him. He had no sense of time, but Travis loved every moment. Every clench of her body made his own sing with intense pleasure.

Kenzie came with intensity. She gripped his shoulders, dug her fingernails into his flesh, and moaned as she rode out her long orgasm. She felt different inside after an orgasm, and he marveled at how soft yet tight she still was after. He held out as long as he could, trying to edge himself as his orgasm surfaced each time, but within a few more minutes, he came, too, and they lay against each other, sweating as the night air cooled their hot skin.

As the night noises returned to his ear, Travis' mind returned to revenge as it always did, and he swallowed the lump forming in his throat. He pulled her closer to him in the dark barn.

Why hadn't he found her before all this was set into motion? Regret made his euphoria short-lived. She napped against his chest, and he held her like he knew she was going to slip away.

CHAPTER 17

Kenzie awoke to light coming in through a crack in the barn wall. She blinked against the light, trying to will her eyes to stay open.

Not a crack.

She closed her eyes. Her head was fuzzy. She reopened them and refocused on the light—a sliver of illumination from dark curtains. Seeing she was on a mattress, she glanced around wildly, realizing she didn't know where she was. She sat up in the bed, but the room was so dark, it was hard to see anything. Kenzie reached out her hand and patted the bed, her fingers contacting warm skin.

Travis.

He breathed deeply as he awoke, almost as if he was startled from a nightmare, and grabbed her hand, pulling her to him in one swift movement with so little effort as if she were all his.

How had he gotten her here? Where was here? His house?

"Where are we?" she asked as he kissed her neck.

"My home, such as it is. It feels more like a house than a home nowadays, though," Travis said and continued his kisses across her collarbone. She felt the familiar tug of desire from deep within as he moved his rough hand across her breast and down her side before cupping it under one buttock. "You still smell like rain."

Kenzie remembered the storm. "And hay, too?"

He laughed. "A little. You were so worn out, you didn't even wake when I carried you home after the rain stopped. I knew you needed rest, and I wanted to give you a comfortable bed to sleep in."

"Why is it so dark in here? What time is it?" She yawned and stretched her arms overhead.

"I have blackout curtains on the windows. I can't stand the sunlight when I'm trying to sleep." Travis picked up his phone, and the glow illuminated his face for a moment. "It's 9:32."

"I need to get back to my car and get home. My roommate's gonna be worried about me."

"Roommate?" His voice had deepened, and there was an edge of danger to it.

"Lena."

The sudden tension in his body melted away. "Or you could stay here, and I could make you come again. And then, I could bring you breakfast in bed."

"Ugh," she said as she squeezed her thighs together against the drumbeat of horniness, "it's truly tempting, but I need..." He was licking her right nipple already, and she let out a groan as the hand that had been cupping her ass glided smoothly to her pussy. A thought occurred to her. "How about I try to get away, and you make me stay and demand that I come for you before I can leave?" She grinned into the darkness as she felt his cock harden against her thigh.

"Fuck yes," Travis said, his voice deep with desire. "I like to play." He jumped up from the bed and rummaged around for a moment. In the dim light, she saw Travis slide on a skeleton mask.

Kenzie grinned and then remembered she was playing a part. She gave him a look of terror. "Why did you bring me here? You're a stranger. Get your hands off me," she began as he pushed open her thighs roughly. She pushed at his hand as his fingers slid against her already wet pussy.

"I'm going to fuck you so good, you're going to beg me to never stop." He pressed his thumb against her clit and then pushed it inside her. Her hips rose to meet his thumb, even as she tried to turn over to get away from him. He pulled her roughly back down the bed to him. "And I won't stop slamming inside you until your cum is dripping down my balls." He was suddenly on top of her and sliding his erection against her pussy. Though he wasn't in her yet, she felt his balls slapping her ass as she fought against him. Travis grabbed her wrists, pinning them to the bed, and try as she might, she couldn't move. He had her legs pinned with his own. Kenzie was immobilized, and she was loving every delicious second of it. She ached with need.

"I'll scream!"

"Good," Travis said. "There's no one anywhere near here, and that'll make me fuck you harder. I like it when you scream, vixen."

When Travis guided his dick into her with only his hips, she screamed, and he rammed it in hard, taking her breath away. She was soaked, but he filled her so wonderfully that she thought she might already be able to come. She shivered from the thrill of his cock filling her and pumping into her over and over and also from the scenario. Apparently, she liked her sex dangerous. She'd never realized that before she met Travis. He'd awakened something dark inside of her that she never knew existed.

"Come for me, you dirty bitch."

Kenzie bit into his shoulder and tried not to come yet. She loved the dirty talk so much that she forgot they were role-playing for a moment and wrapped her legs around him to pull him in even deeper.

He pulled out of her, and she groaned in frustration. "Turn over. Fucking now!" he yelled.

Kenzie's heart hammered in her chest, and she did as he said.

Travis pulled her ass back so that her knees were up near her elbows, with her ass sticking up like they were about to play leapfrog. "Face down, ass up."

He entered her pussy as he pressed against her shoulders, and again, she couldn't move. And the feeling was so deep and wonderful from this angle. This wasn't your normal doggy-style fucking. He ground into her pussy like his life depended on it. "Come for me, or I'll spank your ass like the naughty bitch you've been this weekend."

Before she could respond, he let up from pressing down on her shoulders to give her a stinging smack against her right ass cheek. Kenzie yelped in surprise. He wrapped a hand around the back of her neck and stuck the thumb of his other hand against her asshole, giving it just enough pressure to send shockwaves to her pussy.

"Scream for me, beautiful," Travis pleaded.

She bit into the covers on the bed as she tried to hold off, but she no longer could. She shuddered with a powerful orgasm as she screamed and laughed into the mattress. It was a giddy, nearly hysterical feeling, another sexual first for her.

He came, too, lifting her off the bed with each pulse of his ecstasy. Travis fell to the bed beside her and pulled her to him as he kissed her head and hugged her. "You are fucking amazing."

CHAPTER 18

When her heartbeat finally slowed enough for her to think straight again, Kenzie asked if she could clean up. She was still trembling and covered in sweat.

"Of course," Travis said as he pulled the chain on a lamp beside the bed. She found herself in a large bedroom painted dark blue. They lay on a massive king-sized bed in the middle of the room against the wall farthest from the windows, which were floor-to-ceiling and covered in blue curtains with some kind of print that she couldn't make out in the dim light. He got up and held out a hand for her.

Kenzie's eyes couldn't help but go directly to his dick, which was at eye-level and still partially erect. It was thick and beautiful. She glanced up at his face, which she'd barely seen before now. Travis' scars still shocked her in the light, but she refused to let him see it again. She gave him a smile instead as he pulled her up and led her by the hand to the en suite bathroom.

"Shower?" he asked.

The clawfoot tub looked inviting, but she needed to get home. She nodded, and Travis turned on the water for her. His eyes traveled over her body as she stepped into the warm spray, and his look of appreciation made her smile. He left her there as the steam rose around her. Kenzie pulled a blue washcloth from a shelf just outside of the shower and lathered up with the blue bar of soap in the soap cubby. It smelled manly and fresh, and she wanted the shower to last forever.

Her body was achy, more so than she'd realized, and she allowed the warm water to thrum against her tired muscles for a few extra minutes before she turned off the water and grabbed a towel to dry off. Her pussy, and probably her legs, too, would be sore for days. She smirked. A gift to remember him by.

Kenzie wrapped the towel around her and looked for her costume, not that she wanted to put it back on after getting clean, but what else did she have to wear home? When she stepped back into the bedroom, she found that Travis had laid out a college t-shirt, the same college she attended, she noted with curiosity, a gray thermal shirt to go over it, and a pair of black joggers, which she knew would be too big. She put the clothes on, thankful for them despite their ill fit, and towel-dried her hair before hanging the towel up in the bathroom. She found her boots and pulled them on. They didn't exactly go with her outfit, but beggars can't be choosers, her dad always said.

Kenzie didn't know what she expected when she opened the door to the hallway, but it wasn't to find herself on the second floor overlooking a gigantic crystal chandelier that hung down into the first floor. A staircase curved down either side of the chandelier. *This is a mansion,* she thought as she made her way down one side of the staircase. She could smell food cooking, and her stomach growled in anticipation. She followed her nose to a bright, spacious kitchen where Travis, who'd pulled on a pair of gray sweatpants, buttered toast at the island. The muscles in his arms and back rippled as he worked.

"Do you like jelly?" he asked without looking up at her. He quickly turned away from her and opened the refrigerator. "I'm afraid I don't have a lot in here. Just some grape and apple. I don't cook often. This is my least favorite room in the house." He glanced at her. "It's too bright."

"No jelly."

"If you want scrambled, I can do that, too," he said. Eggs sizzled in a skillet on the stove, and he turned his attention to them, plating the sunny-side-up eggs perfectly without busting a yolk.

"Fried is fine." Kenzie would eat whatever he gave her just to spend more time with him before going home.

Travis barely looked at her. He was busy making breakfast, but she got the sense that he was avoiding her gaze. She wondered if he was more self-conscious here. It seemed like it. So she moved to face him after he deposited each plate on the island, wrapped her hands around his waist, and looked straight into his beautiful, thickly lashed green eyes. "Thank you. The shower was wonderful. I appreciate the warm clothes and the meal."

Travis smiled down at her, but there was a haunted look in his eyes. "You look different, you know, as a normal woman instead of a monster's bride."

"So you like monsters better?" she teased.

"No." He stepped back. He was so hard to read. She realized his dark hair was wet. He'd gotten a shower somewhere else in the house. "Sorry, I don't have any juice," Travis said. "I didn't think to add it to the list. I have someone pick up groceries for me." He turned to the fridge and grabbed a bottle of water, which he put beside her plate.

"It's fine." Kenzie sat down and dug in, eating every bit of the eggs and toast he'd put on her plate. She'd been famished. He watched her with what appeared to be guarded amusement as he picked at his own food.

When she was finished, Kenzie gulped down half of the bottle of water. She hadn't realized how thirsty she was. She wiped at her mouth and grinned. "You dehydrated me with all that sex."

A smile teased his lips, and Kenzie thought she could get accustomed to trying to tease a smile from that mouth. Despite the scars, he was a beautiful specimen of a man. She admired his full lips, solid jaw, the indentions that weren't really dimples on either side of his mouth, which gave him a chiseled look. He had high cheekbones that any girl would be jealous of, but most notable were those intense green eyes under dark lashes. With his broad shoulders and chest and the way his abs trailed down into a V at his waist, he was sexy as hell.

Fuck, this man was beautiful.

If he thought some scars could destroy how handsome he was, he was sadly mistaken.

Travis stood to take her plate, and she grabbed his hand. Without getting off the barstool, she pulled Travis to her and kissed his chest, right where his heart beat. She felt it speed up beneath her lips. "I'm so glad you brought me here. Thank you."

He wrapped his arms around her but said, "I need to take you back to your car." There was regret in his tone, and she felt it, too. Travis kissed the top of her head and picked up her plate. After he deposited it into the sink, he said, "You should feel special. I don't go out in the daylight anymore."

"So you're a vampire?" When he didn't laugh, Kenzie pursed her lips. "What happened to you?"

His green eyes seemed to darken with intensity and anger. "I died. Doctors put me back together, and I had to learn to live again. Or exist, anyway." Travis gave her no more explanation.

Travis led Kenzie into a fancy sitting room, where he pulled on a pullover and sunglasses and handed her a bag with her soiled costume before he grabbed a set of keys and his phone.

Outside, broken limbs and brown leaves littered the yard, but she didn't think all of it had come from the storm last night. It looked like the grounds weren't kept up. In fact, as beautiful as the house was, when she glanced back at it, she noticed a shutter askew and the paint beginning to peel on the front façade. Dead leaves littered the front porch beyond the white columns. The place looked almost haunted. If it hadn't been daylight, it would have definitely given spooky haunted house vibes.

The day was still overcast, and dark clouds threatened more rain as they got into his truck, which he'd parked behind the house. She noticed a pool behind the house, but its water was murky brown. He drove down a long driveway and turned right onto a gravel road, which took them by what she assumed was the barn where they'd spent half the night together. They rode in silence most of the way. Kenzie had so many questions, but she didn't want to pry. He obviously didn't want to talk about what happened to him.

"Listen," he said tentatively as they neared Jameson Farm. She saw his hands tightening against the steering wheel. "It's better if you don't tell anyone about me. Okay? You already know too much." He lifted the hood up so that his face was in shadow.

Kenzie nodded. She realized this might be it. She might never see him again. Their conversation from the night before came back to her. "Don't do whatever you were thinking of doing. I'll stay away from Justin. Just," she paused and gulped against the feeling of her throat closing with emotion, "please, Travis."

"Almost no one knows I'm living out at the old homeplace, and I'd like for it to stay that way for now." Travis kept his eyes on the road and said nothing more until he turned into the vacant parking lot where only her car was parked. He looked around nervously as if expecting someone to be waiting for them. Then, he put the truck in park behind her car but left it idling. "I can't make you any promises. I'm sorry." He turned away from her and looked out his window. "I have to go."

Kenzie grabbed her bag and reached for the door handle. "55 Netherwood Lane. That's where I live. I hope to see you again." She really hoped he'd come to his senses. She pulled the door open without waiting for an answer, afraid that he'd say he wouldn't come, and stepped out into the chill of a mid-October morning. Her hands were trembling, she realized. She could feel Travis' eyes on her with every step she made toward her car, and he waited while she unlocked the door. When Kenzie was inside the car, he drove off like anywhere else was where he'd rather be, spinning gravel behind him, and she had to admit to herself that it stung.

What had she gotten herself into? She felt a tumult of different emotions—desire, frustration, fear, uncertainty, sadness—and it was overwhelming. Kenzie laid her head against the steering wheel and let the tears fall.

CHAPTER 19

"Where were you all night?" Lena sat on the couch, reading a textbook. She smiled and raised an eyebrow. "And whose clothes are those?" Lena looked Kenzie up and down, taking in the large sweats. "Justin's?"

What Travis had asked of her, to not tell anyone about him, crossed her mind before she blurted anything out. Instead, Kenzie said, "I got caught in the storm and stayed at a friend's house." She was so accustomed to telling Lena everything that it felt like she was betraying her friend. She shrugged against the weight of guilt. "It was a weird night." Kenzie took the bag with her sodden clothes to the washing machine and dumped them into it.

Lena called out, "Let me know if you wanna talk about it!"

Kenzie ignored her roommate while she poured in the laundry detergent and turned on the machine before escaping into her room. Of course, she wanted to talk about it. But she couldn't.

Kenzie kicked off her boots, lay down on the bed, and hugged herself, inhaling Travis' smell on his clothes.

She wanted to wear them forever, wallowing in that scent and forgetting whatever else needed to be done for the day. Kenzie couldn't help it; she was smitten with the bad-boy recluse living up in a haunted-ass-looking mansion, though she didn't know what she was going to do about his proclivity for murder. Her stomach was heavy with dread at the thought. Why did Travis have it out for Justin? What had happened between them? Did it have anything to do with whatever accident had scarred him so badly?

"Oh, shit," she heard Lena exclaim from the living room.

Kenzie rolled over as curiosity piqued her interest and squelched the lassitude that had come over her since leaving Travis' house. "What?" She rolled out of bed with a sigh and went into the living room, where Lena stared at her phone.

"Apparently, the fraternity that Justin Reese Greyer is a part of is being targeted. Someone shared a local news article. One of the brothers, Vaughn Armstrong, who's like a state representative's son, has gone missing, and they just found the body of another fraternity brother dead outside the guy's girlfriend's sorority house. Caleb Whitlock, 22, an international business major. He'd been stabbed six times." She looked up at Kenzie, who was barely breathing. Lena's eyes were wide with worry. "Does Justin Reese know what's going on?"

Kenzie shook her head. "I don't know. I haven't talked to him since last night at the Spook Trail."

"They're wondering if Vaughn has something to do with it or if something has happened to him, too. I mean, if two of the brothers are dead, we're looking at a potential serial killer on campus if someone else turns up dead."

Kenzie frowned. That someone could very well be Justin Reese Greyer. Travis had said he was next. Her hands shook.

"You weren't over there last night, were you?"

"No," Kenzie said. It came out high-pitched like a question. "No," she said more resolutely. Had Travis gone looking for Justin and killed a frat brother in a rage instead? Or was this even related to whatever was going on with Travis? "Does it say if the guy got killed last night or this morning?"

"It doesn't say. Just that the body was found this morning. Everyone's talking about it, though, and the President of the college is putting a curfew in place around campus, just in case. I'm so glad we live off campus."

"Me, too," Kenzie mumbled as she went back to her room and sat down at her desk. Her mind kept going back to the pure hatred and violence she'd seen in Travis' eyes the night before when he talked about Justin Reese. It was such a stark contrast to the gentleness and caring he'd shown her this morning. It was almost like two different men.

She opened her laptop, pulled up the news article after a quick search, and scanned it for information, but it didn't give her anything that Lena hadn't already told her.

Kenzie thought about searching for Travis, but she realized she didn't even know his last name. She closed her eyes and put her head in her hands. Who was this guy?

Her eyes popped open. She added Travis and the fraternity plus the college to her search.

Three articles popped up that seemed relevant. One had to do with last year's bid day and who had been invited into the fraternity's chapter on campus. Travis Weber was listed. He was the only Travis on the list.

She adjusted her search for Travis Weber. Some golf pro's face came up, but that wasn't her Travis. A few posts down the page, she found the article she was looking for. Her eyes scanned the news article, which explained that Travis Weber, a local college student, had been found in a rural area by a farmer, already maimed and barely alive. He'd been airlifted to a hospital in Nashville and was in critical condition. There was an ongoing investigation into what'd happened to him. There were no updates to the article, though. Not surprising for the local news.

She navigated back to the search results and found an article that detailed Travis' mother and father's car accident, their obituaries, and an article from several years ago naming Travis as an MVP of a private high school soccer team. Nothing else.

Damn, he'd had an awful life the past several years, losing his family and then going through some kind of accident himself that was so horrific that he had to be pieced back together. Had anyone been there for him through that ordeal? Or did he have to do it all alone? She tried to temper the pity she felt growing in her chest with the fact that he was disturbed enough to want to kill someone. And maybe already had. Kenzie shivered.

"They just found Vaughn Armstrong's truck, and they expect foul play," Lena called from the living room. "Jason, from my sociology class, says it's going to be on the news at noon."

Kenzie and Lena sat down together on the couch and watched the news report. The camera panned the front of the sorority house where the body had been found before showing a shot of the outside of Justin's frat house, where they explained that Caleb Whitlock had been living. They mentioned the disappearance of Vaughn Armstrong and suggested that there might be a connection, but most of it was vague. It didn't give them any more answers. Kenzie slumped back against the couch while Lena turned off the TV.

"Ask Justin what the hell is going on," Lena said.

"I don't know if I should bother him. I bet people are blowing up his phone," Kenzie said. The truth was, she didn't really want to talk to him. Though she felt guilty that Travis had it out for him and she hadn't told him about it, something told her to stay out of it. She didn't know who she should trust right now, and she was sure there was more to the story of Travis' injuries.

"Yeah, but they're not *you*. He'll talk to you," Lena insisted.

Kenzie picked up her phone from the coffee table and pulled up the messages app.

> Everything okay over there? The house is all over the news.

It took Justin a few minutes to respond. She'd laid her phone back down on the table, assuming that he really was too busy to message her back, when it buzzed.

> It's a shitstorm over here. Has been all morning.

> I can imagine. When did it happen?

> The cops think sometime in the middle of the night or early morning.

At least that cleared Travis. She sighed with relief. She'd been with him all night. Though she'd passed out, she admitted. It was odd that she hadn't awakened when he'd carried her into his house from the barn. How had she been that tired? Had he roofied her? Kenzie couldn't imagine what his motive for drugging her would be, though. He could have just left her there in the barn and took off.

She couldn't help wondering if he could have gone to campus and come back before she awoke the next morning. He would've had plenty of time to drive to campus and then come back to the mansion.

Fuck.

Another concern ate at her. Had he taken her to his house to act as his alibi? He told her to tell no one where she was last night, but if it came down to it and the police questioned her about Travis, she could give him the alibi he needed if he became a suspect. Kenzie bit her lip.

> Were you and Caleb close?

> We'd pledged together, so you could say so.

> I'm sorry.

> Do they have any suspects?

I don't think so.

And it's nothing some serious snuggling wouldn't take care of.

> Think I'll pass on coming to campus tonight. I don't want to be the next one murdered.

This isn't a slasher flick.

> Might as well be.

Kenzie paused. She was being insensitive.

> I'm sorry. I'm just a little scared.

> It's so weird.

> They're saying this could be a serial killer.

If you won't risk getting gutted on campus, maybe I'll come to you.

The fuck you will, she thought. Then, she paused. When had she completely changed her mind about Justin? She'd been crazy about him less than a week ago. Was it Travis? Was it all the warnings he'd given her about Justin? Now, she didn't know if she could trust Justin to be the nice guy he appeared to be.

> You mean you aren't abiding by the campus curfew?

> I won't have to break a curfew if I stay at your place.

Kenzie's eyes widened. Justin had invited himself to her place, and she was having second thoughts. His affection had been her goal for so long that it felt wrong to turn him down, but it felt wrong not to, as well. Besides standing there in another man's clothes, she'd rather be spending her time with Travis and getting to know him. Kenzie went to the fridge to pour herself a glass of tea. What was she supposed to tell Justin?

A message came through with a buzz in her palm, and she expected another message from Justin. Instead, it was from a contact she'd never seen before–Monster. Her eyes widened. Travis must have put his number into her phone while she was showering at his house.

> Hi, vixen. I haven't stopped thinking about you.

> Are you working tonight?

> No. It's Sunday, so Jameson's is closed.

:(I would have liked to join you again.

> Where were you last night before you came to the spook trail?

At home.

> What about after you took me inside?

I was by your side all night.

Right where I belonged.

Ugh, why did that last comment do such fluttery things to her heart?

Kenzie bit her lip. Could she believe him? Maybe he was a killer and a pathological liar. She knew him intimately, yet barely knew him at all. That scared her.

I'm looking at your house. And since your car is in the driveway, I'm guessing you're home.

Kenzie jumped up and ran to the front window. Sure enough, she saw Travis' truck down the street. He was only a dark figure from this distance. She gulped.

> I kept replaying the address you gave me through my head, and before I knew it, I was here.

If Lena met Travis, she'd bombard Kenzie with questions. And maybe she'd start putting two and two together as Kenzie had, and that might put her friend's life in danger. Fuck, was she seriously considering going back out with the guy who she was afraid might kill her best friend? What the hell had she gotten herself into?

> K: Don't come up. Lena is home, and she's far too nosey for her own good.

Lena came out of the kitchen just then and saw Kenzie at the window. "What's up?" She strode over and glanced out the window. "Are the neighbors fighting in the front yard again?"

"No," Kenzie said as she backed away from the window. "I thought I heard something. I think it was a vehicle backfiring." She sat back down on the couch as nonchalantly as possible and pulled her messages back up.

> I hadn't planned on it. Meet me?

> Where?

> Somewhere no one will likely be at night.

> Riverside Cemetery.

Kenzie gulped. Did she really want to meet a guy in a graveyard who liked to wear masks and wanted to kill her sort-of boyfriend? Okay, so Justin hadn't so much as taken her on a date yet... *Focus, Kenzie!* Travis could have already hurt her if he'd wanted to. He didn't likely have nefarious reasons for meeting her now.

> 7?

> See you then.

Kenzie needed to make sure Justin didn't show up at her door tonight. That would complicate things. As she was pulling up the message with Justin, he sent her another one.

> Kenz?

> Can't tonight.

> Why is that?

> I feel like you're hot and cold with me lately. What gives?

> I've got family stuff tonight. I'll see you in class.

> Sure.

> Save me a seat.

"I'm thinking about going to visit my parents tonight. I'll probably spend the night, so don't wait up," Kenzie said as she stood. She didn't enjoy lying to Lena, but if Justin showed up anyway, Lena would back up her story.

Now, she could concentrate on who she really wanted to spend time with. She went to her room to change.

CHAPTER 20

Kenzie parked her car along the street underneath the immense oak trees lining the side of the cemetery flanked by the road. She pulled on her red corduroy coat and got out of her car, feeling less brave now that she was actually about to walk through a graveyard at night. Travis' truck wasn't parked on the street, so she assumed he'd parked inside the cemetery.

She walked down the narrow lane that wound its way through the large cemetery. A gust of wind blew up dead leaves in front of her, and they swirled as if animated by some unheard song before settling back to the ground. Her own grandparents were buried here, and she knew the cemetery pretty well. In the daylight, it was a peaceful place. At night, though, it was too quiet. The twittering of birds ceased, and even the crickets and frogs seemed too reverent to make much noise here after dark.

"Kenzie," a low, deep voice said to her right. Even without seeing him, she knew it was Travis. And the timbre of his voice made her knees weak. He was sitting on the steps of a stone mausoleum that glowed a gray-white in the weak moonlight.

When the thudding of her heart slowed, she said, "Hi." Kenzie turned and headed toward him. "Why here, Travis? Isn't it a little morbid? I could have come out to your house again."

"I didn't think you'd want to drive all the way out there again."

Honestly, she'd want to go wherever he was. She didn't say that out loud, though, for fear that he'd think she was crazy. Maybe she *was* crazy. He had a powerful hold on her in such a short time. She'd never fallen for someone so hard and so fast. All she wanted was to be near him, and though she didn't think it was all that healthy, she couldn't help her feelings.

Travis stood. He held something behind his back, and she wondered for a moment if it was the knife he'd brought to the Spook Trail. Her heart thundered in her chest, and she wondered if he could hear it. If he was going to stab her, would he kill her here right out in the open?

"I like this place," he said. "I come here sometimes to think. And to visit my parents." He gestured with a nod of his head behind him at the mausoleum.

"Oh," she said. "I'm sorry." Kenzie moved toward him, forgetting her fear for a moment. She wanted to comfort him, but she didn't know how.

Travis swung his arm from behind his back. Kenzie gasped. He thrust a single purple rose toward her.

"Oh!" Kenzie said. It was perfectly formed and delicate, and when she took it and raised it to her nose, its scent was heady. "Thank you. It's beautiful."

"So are you," Travis said, his voice deepening with emotion.

Kenzie rose up on her tiptoes and kissed his cheek with the scar along his jaw. She breathed in the fresh scent of his soap mixed with the warmth of leather and wood, just like his clothes she'd left in her room. No way was he getting those back.

"Until recently, I thought I wanted to join them."

Kenzie felt her heart swell with sorrow for him. "What happened to you?"

"There was an accident. At least, I think it was an accident. Maybe it wasn't." Travis shook his head, and she saw his eyes gleaming with fresh tears. "They left me there like I was no better than roadkill." He turned away from her. "I had no one. I was utterly alone."

Kenzie put her hand on the small of his back to pull him closer. She wished with just her touch that she could take his pain away. Travis turned suddenly and wrapped himself around her.

"God, your touch feels so good, so comforting. I'd forgotten that feeling. My entire existence has been a torment to me this past year. The pain, the loneliness, the anger that radiated through me every waking moment. None of it felt good. It was chaos.

"Then, I ran into this wild, gorgeous, stubborn woman in the woods who looked as pieced together as I was. The anguish melted away as you thawed my heart. In only a few days, you made me see that there was something worth living for. I know that sounds irrational, but it's true."

Kenzie shook her head. "I feel it, too," she whispered.

"I was a decent man before the accident, but misery made me a monster. Happiness has made me want to be honorable again." Travis looked into her eyes as if searching for something to save him. "I've been awful. I've done bad things—things I can't even tell you."

"You don't have to." And she meant it. Kenzie didn't have to know any more about Travis to know that she was enamored with him. As far as she was concerned, any mistakes he made in the past were behind them.

"I'm going to have to leave for a while," Travis said.

A fresh ache crept into her heart. "Why?"

He gave her a look so intense that her heart stuttered. Because of whatever he'd done, she thought. He's got to disappear for a while. Kenzie sighed. "Then, let's spend one more night together before you leave. Let me get my fill of you, if that's even possible."

"I'll never get my fill of you." He smashed his lips into hers. It was a hot, passionate kiss that promised the falsehood that tomorrow would never come.

CHAPTER 21

Kenzie followed behind Travis' truck out through the countryside and past Jameson Farm to the Weber estate. At night, the mansion looked even more forlorn and haunted in the gloom. It was the kind of house she and her high school friends might have trespassed to get inside to spend a few hours on a dark autumn night for the thrill.

A different kind of thrill raced through her as she stepped out of her car and walked toward Travis.

Travis reached back and took her hand as he climbed the front steps.

"Welcome to my lair," he said in a low, raspy voice with wide eyes and a grin.

Kenzie laughed and smacked him on the arm with her other hand. "I've been in your lair before, and I liked it." His playfulness did things to her body that she couldn't ignore. Even the simple act of holding her hand, like he was claiming her as his, was enough to make her want to pant with desire.

"True, but I never got to welcome you. Or give you a tour."

Travis barely got the words out before her mouth was on his. She couldn't wait any longer. She wanted to be all over him—to open him up and step inside him. That's how close she wanted to be. She pushed him against the wall and pressed her body into his as she licked into his mouth.

"Oh," he groaned into the kiss. "Fuck the tour."

Kenzie pulled at the button of his jeans without moving her mouth from his. She thought she'd never taste him again, and he was all hers tonight. "This is the kind of welcome I prefer," she said as she took a step back, dropped her coat on the floor, and pulled off her sweater.

Travis pulled her back to him. His hands roamed up and down her torso like he didn't know what he wanted to touch most. One hand squeezed her breast, while the other grabbed at her ass, pulling her closer to him. She ran her fingers into his hair as he kissed her neck. Kenzie sighed with delight. He pressed his hardness into her. In a flash, his pants were down, and he kicked them behind her. Then, he yanked hers down and turned her toward the wall. Standing behind her now, he pressed his cock against her ass cheeks, but she still had her panties on.

"Are you wet for me yet?" he whispered into her ear. He slid his hand into her panties and stroked her clit. "Ah, so wet and ready for me."

Kenzie grinned. She loved the sound of his voice, especially when he whispered things like that to her. Pressing her ass against him and wiggling, she tried to entice him to take her. She wanted so badly for him to hurry up and rip off her panties and fuck her like she needed. "Please," she begged.

"Not yet, my little vixen." He slipped his fingers inside her and then smoothed her wetness across her already throbbing clit. Back and forth, he pulled her quickly to the edge. Only a few seconds later, she was clawing at the wall and trying to turn to face him. Kenzie needed him inside her. She needed the fullness of him, the strokes of pleasure, and the intensity of all the sensations combined. And as he slipped back and forth against her hot pussy and her throbbing clit, she knew she'd come soon if he didn't stop.

"That's a good girl," he said as he flicked his tongue at her earlobe, which sent another twinge of pleasure straight to her pussy.

Kenzie moaned with frustration. She didn't want to waste an orgasm on his fingers when his dick could give her so much more pleasure. "Stop!"

Travis let up, but he didn't let go of her.

"I need you inside me," Kenzie pleaded.

Kenzie needed the kind of electricity that only Travis had ever provided. She'd never felt the jolt of pleasure he gave her with orgasms. Sex with him was otherworldly. It was electric.

Kenzie reached behind her and stroked his cock with her hand, willing him to act on his promises. It worked. He pulled her panties down as she turned to face him. He picked her up and entered her in one swift thrust. She gasped at the sudden fullness. He pressed her against the wall, and she wrapped her legs around his waist.

"I want all of you," he said as he bucked, pushing his entire length into her again and again. One arm was around her waist, and the other hand was in her hair. "I want you every day and forever."

Kenzie rode his cock as fervently as she rode the high his words gave her. He lowered her to the floor and raised her legs to rest on his shoulders as he drove as deep as he could into her, as if he, too, wanted to climb inside her and reside.

That wonderful wave of pleasure hit her, and her eyes rolled back in her head as the biggest wave hit her. Kenzie clutched at his forearms as she cried out.

"That's right, beautiful. Scream for me."

Kenzie howled a guttural cry as she bucked with the last few waves of pleasure.

"Perfect, vixen. Now, my turn," Travis said and kissed her as she panted. Travis turned her to the side so that only one leg was raised, and he fucked her fast and hard. "Mmm," he said, "you're so swollen now. I love that fucking feeling. It's like heaven."

In no time, he grunted with his own orgasm, thrusting inside her with each pulse of his dick. Without pulling out, he lay beside her and pulled her into an embrace.

CHAPTER 22

"I want to show you something." Travis took her hand and guided her into the next room without turning the lights on. Kenzie suspected that he rarely had them on, that he liked sitting in the darkness in this big ol' house by himself. He guided her through the rooms, his grip on her hand firm and comforting.

Both of them were still naked. The chill in the air pebbled her nipples and gave her goosebumps. They came to a room with a baby grand piano, two couches, and a few chairs.

"This is the music room. In my youth, I spent a lot of time here." He motioned to one of the couches, and she curled up on it and wrapped her arms around her legs for warmth while he stooped in front of a fireplace. Soon, the gas logs were blazing with flames, and warmth filled the room.

In the golden-orange glow of the fire, he looked monstrous as shadows leaped across his face and the muscles of his chest and legs, highlighting the scars that marred his body. And he was exquisite. She could have stared at him all night. He noticed her appreciative gaze and smirked with a mixture of humor and bashfulness that she found incredibly sexy.

Kenzie was no longer afraid of this man. He was damaged, but he cared for her. That much she knew to be true.

Kenzie glanced at the hulking piano. "Do you play?" Kenzie asked.

"No. Well, a little, but it's nothing special. My mother could make me weep with her playing, though. She was very talented."

Kenzie tried to imagine little Travis sitting there watching his mother as her fingers glided gracefully across the keys. It must have killed him when she died.

Kenzie turned her attention back to the man in front of her. She watched him move about in the darkness. She realized there was a large instrument on a stand near the piano as he reached it and picked it up.

"I played alongside my mother from the time I was about seven. Of course, I wasn't using a full-size cello back then." He picked up the bow from an open case and sat down with the instrument between his legs. It was large enough to cover up most of his body. "Up until a few days ago, I hadn't played this in years. To play music is to feel alive, and I hadn't truly felt alive in a long while." His voice was quiet, almost reverent. He placed his bow against the strings and moved the fingers of his other hand to the strings on the neck. In the dim light, he must have known instinctively where he wanted to start. "You made me want to play again."

Travis moved the bow across the strings, and a deep, sad music filled the room. It flowed around her and tugged at her heart. The notes soon rose higher, giving the song a sense of hope and lightness. Then, the pacing sped up to a frenetic energy that gave her a sense of urgency before it slowed again. Up and down, the energy went as the song continued. The muscles of his arms and shoulders stretched and rippled with the flow of music. Travis wore an expression of concentration mixed with joy. The way he moved with the instrument was fascinating to watch. He was feeling the music as much as she was.

Tears sprang to her eyes. It was absolutely beautiful.

He was absolutely beautiful.

When he finished, silence filled the room. It was amazing how loud the silence was in the absence of music.

"That was Sonata No. 3. Sonatas are meant to be played alongside the piano. It was my mother's favorite, and we played it together often."

Kenzie found it hard to speak, to clear the emotion from her voice. "Thank you for sharing that with me."

"Here's a fun one, if you're enjoying it." As wonderfully as he played, he sounded unsure of himself.

"Immensely. Please continue."

"This one can be played with a quartet, but I like playing the melody. See if you recognize it."

As soon as he produced the first few notes, Kenzie recognized it as "Creep" by Radiohead. She'd never considered how sorrowful it would sound on a stringed instrument. She shook her head in amazement as he continued. His playing was captivating to watch.

When Travis finished the song, he looked up at her with a look so forlorn that she wanted to embrace him. It made her heart twinge with pity.

"Don't stop. Let me hear one more."

Travis nodded. "You might recognize this one, too."

Travis placed his bow against the strings, moving his fingers back to the neck of the instrument. Kenzie nodded as she instantly recognized it from "The Phantom of the Opera." It was one of her favorite movies. She smiled and listened to him play, getting lost in the music and imagining her favorite moments from the movie. Music transports the listener in that way. With its ability to pull out emotional associations, it's an intimate time machine.

"It's amazing what horse hairs against metal strings can do," he said quietly once he'd finished the song.

"Lovely. I never realized how interesting an instrument a cello is before now. I love that song, by the way."

Travis smiled. "I thought you might. You strike me as a fan of old, gothic buildings and scary, dangerous men in masks."

Kenzie laughed. "Well, now that you say it out loud, that might be where my mask kink started. Erik was intriguing."

Travis laughed a deep, hearty chuckle that made her grin. She wanted to make him laugh often. Most of all, she realized she wanted to make him happy again.

That night, Travis made love to her in his bed. No kinks. No games. No manic screwing.

Kisses, caresses, heat, and intensity—wonderfully sensual intimacy. She fell asleep in his strong arms.

CHAPTER 23

Kenzie awoke to a ding on her phone. She reached over to the bedside table where she'd placed it the night before. It was almost four in the morning. Who would text her so early? She blinked the blurriness from her eyes and pulled up her messages, which were from Lena.

> Let me know you're okay.

> I'm fine. Why?

> Call me.

Kenzie reached over to Travis, but he wasn't in the bed. Dread filled her stomach, but she didn't know if it was because he was gone or because something was wrong with Lena.

Kenzie tapped Lena's picture and hit "call."

"Okay, so when I got off work at midnight," Lena began without so much as a hello to her, "I drove by campus on my way home. There were cop cars, paramedics, and students everywhere."

"Why? And I thought the campus was on a curfew."

"A curfew goes to hell when there's another murder on campus."

Kenzie's stomach dropped. "Oh, no."

"Yeah, so I stopped to see what I could find out. Rumors were flying everywhere, but all I could ascertain was that a female student's body had been found close to campus in an alley dumpster that had been set on fire."

Kenzie's mouth watered as if she might be sick. She put her hand against her stomach. "Ugh, that's awful. Was she burned alive? Or do they think she was killed before?" Kenzie asked.

"I don't know. Maybe dumped. Who knows? You know they'll have to do an autopsy if there's enough left to autopsy. But it's so tragic. Here I was thinking someone was going after frat guys, and hey, who am I to question that? They're all douche canoes. But, apparently, this has become a full-blown killing spree."

Kenzie said, "I thought serial killers followed a pattern, like thin, dark-haired women in their 30s or something."

"Not the ones who get away with it."

***

Kenzie heard the commotion of male voices coming from outside the mansion. She threw on her clothes in a hurry, raced down the stairs, and stopped at the door to listen. She heard Travis' voice mixed with another male's voice.

"Why are you still alive?" a voice shouted.

Was that... Justin's voice?

"You're psychotic," Travis said. "You've had it out for me for years. I don't know why. What have I ever had that you didn't have yourself, you spoiled fucker?"

"I don't feel anything, which you'd never get because you feel too much. You let emotion rule you, Travis. You always have. That's why you fucked up and killed Sam tonight, and you'll go down for *all* these murders."

Who was Sam? Was it short for a Samantha, by chance? Could Travis have left and set the woman on fire near campus in the time that Kenzie had been asleep? She grimaced at the thought, but deep down, she didn't believe it. Or wouldn't.

Kenzie opened the front door and stepped onto the front porch. She needed answers. She couldn't be with a man who continued to murder people, for fuck's sake. Stomach acid threatened to come up, and she swallowed it back down.

Please don't be the campus murderer, she silently prayed.

"You shouldn't have sent your henchman out here to spy on me," Travis said through clenched teeth. "That's why he's dead. More fucking blood on your hands."

Kenzie sucked in air. Travis just admitted that he'd killed someone, but it wasn't the girl from campus. How could she keep defending him when she knew he was murdering people? Didn't that make her an accomplice or something? It felt like her heart was breaking.

She stepped toward Travis but stopped as she noticed Justin glaring at her.

"Are you fucking kidding me right now?" Justin took a step forward. "Kenzie?" His eyes were wide with surprise. "You lied to me," Justin said.

Kenzie ignored him and looked at Travis. "Did you kill someone tonight?" Tears fell as she watched guilt flit across his beautiful features.

Travis turned away.

"Answer me," she whispered.

"What are you doing, Kenzie? Do you even know the kind of man you've gotten entangled with?" Justin asked.

"It was self-defense," Travis said to her. "The guy broke into my house. I couldn't let him hurt you or me. I had no choice. He had a tire iron in his hands. When he swung at me, I stabbed him."

Kenzie looked down and realized he was covered in blood and dirt. Travis had obviously already buried the guy. While she slept in his bed, he'd killed and buried a guy. She felt lightheaded. She needed to sit. If it was self-defense, wasn't it understandable? But if it was self-defense, why did Travis bury the body? She shook her head, confused.

She could barely see him through tears that threatened to fall. He looked down at her for a moment more before turning his eyes back to Justin.

"I had a fucking feeling in my gut. Fuck, I knew something was off. I hadn't heard from you after the... *accident*." The way he said the word made Kenzie think it left a bad taste in his mouth. "We were all surprised that you survived that shit, you know. Then, you didn't tell the police what really happened that night. That surprised the hell outta me. And when I drove out here to see you finally, the house was shut up. Maybe you were still in rehab, but I figured you'd left town for good. That is, until Vaughn went missing. I had my suspicions." Justin's eyes narrowed as he turned them toward Kenzie. "Then, my girl here starts sending me weird texts, and she stops throwing herself at me. I was having so much fun playing with her. So, I had to come see for myself if you were back, if you were behind all this." His mouth became a hard, thin line.

Travis moved Kenzie behind himself as if to shield her from Justin.

"I just didn't expect Kenzie to be out here fucking you. I can't believe how right my hunches were." Justin peered around Travis to look Kenzie in the eyes. "You're a whore, Kenzie. You're fucking a monster, you know that? He's a killer, and nothing's going to change that. Travis isn't worth the air he breathes." Though his words seethed with anger, Justin stood motionless, as if he were having a casual conversation with them.

Kenzie, though, was so filled with rage that she saw red. How dare he call her names with the reputation he had around campus? And how dare he run Travis into the ground? He wasn't half the man Travis was. She could tell that in the short time she'd known him. If anything, *that* caused Justin's apparent jealousy of Travis. People could see what a piece of shit he was when he was held up beside a guy like Travis. She tensed up and clenched her fists, but Travis held out an arm to stop her from going at Justin.

Travis stepped forward. "Shut your fucking mouth. You don't talk to her that way. Say what you want about me, but don't you say one bad word about Kenzie."

"Or what?"

"Or you'll see just how much of a killer I am," Travis said with a menacing growl.

Justin pulled out a pistol from the back of his pants. "You gonna try to take a cheap shot at me again like you did at that party when I fucked Bee?" He raised the gun and pointed it straight at Travis' chest. Kenzie screamed as Travis moved backward, bumping into her and knocking her off her feet. Kenzie fell to the ground and scrambled to the right to get away from Justin.

Justin sneered at Travis, clearly enjoying the reaction of fear. "I won't wait for you to strike first this time. I should've killed you years ago. I would've saved myself so much grief."

Justin pulled the trigger.

Kenzie screamed and covered her ears instinctively against the sound even as she saw the jolt of the bullet push Travis back, hitting him on the right side of his body. He stumbled and fell against the front steps of the mansion.

Kenzie knelt beside him. Travis grimaced against the pain as he held his shoulder, blood pouring from the wound. "Get out of here, vixen," Travis said through clenched teeth. "He's not going to walk away this time."

This time? she wondered. Kenzie glanced up as Justin advanced on them, the gun still pointed in their direction. "Fuck!" She gave Travis' hand a squeeze and let go.

Terrified, she stood and ran, hoping Justin wouldn't put a bullet in her back. If he followed her, though, maybe Travis could get away.

Justin fired again, but she didn't know if it was at her or at Travis again. Kenzie ran as fast as she could, adrenaline coursing through her. She was thankful she hadn't caught a bullet in the back as she continued to round the house.

Please don't be dead, Kenzie thought.

She ran past the back of the house and tore across the lawn into the trees beyond the backyard, and she kept running until her lungs burned and felt like they were going to give out. Small limbs slapped at her face, and she stumbled through the underbrush, fallen limbs, and drift of old leaves and pine needles.

At one point, she heard someone thrashing through the trees and brush, and she was almost certain it was Justin. He was coming for her, and she had to run or hide. She felt like a hunted animal looking for a place to burrow.

Kenzie spotted a rotten tree in the moonlight that had fallen in a heap to the forest floor, half decomposed, and she circled around it to where she was mostly concealed by the greenery of a thick cedar. She hunched down and made herself as small as she could.

Kenzie tried desperately to stop the heaving of her chest and lungs. More than the running, she was suffocating under the weight of leaving Travis lying there on the steps. She closed her eyes and prayed that if Justin had run after her, Travis got away from the house.

A whimper escaped her mouth, and she clamped it shut with both her hands. *Don't break down yet*, she told herself. She squeezed her eyes shut against the image of him lying there, shot. When she opened her eyes, she saw the sky lighting up an odd orange hue. It was still too early for dawn by more than an hour. Then, she realized what it must be.

No, please, no. Fire.

Justin was burning down the house. He'd probably shot Travis again and pulled the body inside before dousing it with gasoline. She thought she might be sick. Tears streamed down her face as she made her way back toward the house. She had to see for herself, but she couldn't risk getting too close. If Travis was dead, she was a witness to murder, and Justin might kill her for it. In fact, she was sure he'd come for her, too.

What a fucking mess she'd stepped into.

PART 2

"When falsehood can look so like the truth, who can assure themselves of certain happiness?"

"The fallen angel becomes a malignant devil. Yet even that enemy of God and man had friends and associates in his desolation; I am alone."

-Mary Shelley, *Frankenstein*

CHAPTER 24

Five Years Later

Kenzie stared at the email from earlier that morning. Dillon Books, the publishing company that hired her right out of college a couple of years ago, was merging with another company, details to be forthcoming, it had said. It left her uneasy, especially if they were glossing over the fact that this could be an acquisition where the takeover company could completely consume Dillon Books. That would mean a huge amount of change.

Would her boss remain the same? She liked Mr. Herschinger. He gave her the editing position when she had very little experience under her belt because he saw her talent for finding the structural flaws in stories and being able to intuitively offer suggestions for how to fix them and for her quick editing skills. Would they make cuts to jobs or hire a lot of new people that she'd have to get to know?

She fanned herself with her hand. Why was it suddenly so hot in her office? Maybe she was having a heart attack at the ripe old age of twenty-four.

It was strange how quickly a person's sense of security could get rocky. She pulled out the bottle of antacid tablets from her desk drawer and chewed on the minty medicine. Kenzie didn't take big changes well. And there had been enough distractions throughout the day that she'd gotten very little actual work done.

"Makenzie, you heading out soon?" Sonja Kellerman asked as she stopped at Kenzie's office door. Sonja was ten years her senior and had been somewhat of a big sister to her in the company. Kenzie didn't think she'd have made it through her initial internship with the company if not for Sonja's wise guidance and mentoring. She and Sonja sometimes walked together through the parking garage late at night for extra safety. Because they both were often there late, they'd been doing that for years.

The city was dangerous. Well, anywhere can be dangerous, even her own little cozy college town, which she'd moved away from soon after the campus killings. Kenzie had learned long ago to keep a weapon on her, but she'd much rather deter someone from even approaching her than to have to use it on someone. She didn't have the stomach for killing.

The volume in Sonja's dark hair had fallen flat, and she was getting shadows under her eyes. They'd all been working hard, but Sonja was a beast in the business. She was usually here before everyone else in the mornings.

Kenzie's eyes settled on the files in front of her. "I should, but no, I have too much left to do." She gave a disgusted face. "Have you heard yet which company we're merging with?"

Sonja pursed her lips. "Nope, they're keeping it a secret. Hopefully, we'll know more after tomorrow's meeting. Don't look so glum. This merger could really strengthen Dillon Books and put us at the forefront of the publishing industry. It's been languishing for several years now. This is a positive thing." Sonja knew what was on Kenzie's mind without having to ask because the news was on everyone's mind right now.

"Maybe," Kenzie said without enthusiasm. She appreciated Sonja's positivity, but she didn't feel any better. "Be careful, and have a good night."

Sonja waved a few fingers as she headed toward the elevator.

Kenzie heard the wind whipping around the building, reminding her that autumn would soon turn to frightfully cold winter.

She'd continued her degree in the city where she knew no one, keeping her head down and working hard to finish in three more semesters. After graduating near the top of her class, she lucked out on an internship at a publishing firm, where she proved herself and got a full-time position just two years after she graduated. She loved her job, and she was satisfied with her life—except on nights like tonight when the cold was settling in and the sky was black and moonless. It was close to Halloween, which always made her think about home, about college, and about Travis. And those were memories best kept buried.

Kenzie tapped her fingers against the back of her phone, contemplating messaging her friend with benefits, Mark Flores. He could warm her up on this chilly October night if he was free. She frowned and removed her fingers before she picked up the phone. Mark was becoming boring. Hell, if she was honest, he'd been boring all along. Though he had a body like a naughty Greek god, sex with him was so vanilla. It's why they'd never gotten past the friends part in their little trysts over the past six months. She'd tried to encourage him with a little dom and sub fun, but he wanted to be dominated, which surprised her, and that really wasn't her thing. She'd much rather *be* dominated. Getting fucked by a masked man in the middle of the woods flashed through her mind. Kenzie shivered, but she wasn't sure if it was from a wave of pleasure or fear that the memory caused.

What she needed was a drink after work to warm her before she headed home. The thought of a glass of whisky made her think of her dad, whom she hadn't called in a while. Though she'd vowed to leave drinking alone long ago, she'd given up on that resolution after the horrors she experienced at college. She refused to keep it in her apartment, though. That would make drinking too easily accessible until it became a nightly ritual that she'd need to fall asleep. No, she wouldn't become an alcoholic. At least if the alcohol was only at the bar, she could talk herself out of going some of the time.

Kenzie busied herself typing notes about the current manuscript she'd received chapters of this week. Then, she picked through a few more submissions, most of which she added to her slush pile after only a few pages in. Kenzie pinched the bridge of her nose. Her eyes were tired and watering, and she needed food. After grabbing her coat and purse, she headed to the parking garage.

Kenzie kept her purse close to her body and walked briskly to her car, her heels clicking loudly against the concrete. Her autumn coat was too thin for the night. She shivered against the cold draft that swept through the garage. Few cars were left at this late hour. She held her keys in her hand, and her thumb was on the pepper spray button attached to her keyring. There was a handgun in her purse, but she didn't think she could get to it fast enough if someone surprised her. That was why it was imperative to be extra vigilant.

She stopped walking and glanced over her shoulder, almost sure she'd heard someone behind her and to her right. With no one in sight, she picked up her pace, willing herself not to break into a run. She didn't need a twisted or broken ankle from getting the heebie-jeebies alone at night. Plus, she lived alone, so she couldn't give in to fear, or it would consume her.

Her heart was pounding when Kenzie made it to her car. She clicked unlock on her key fob just as she grabbed at the door handle. She glanced in the back seat as she always did before settling into the driver's seat and locking the doors. Relieved, she let out a whoosh of air. She pushed her key into the ignition when a dark shadow fell across her.

A man suddenly pressed against her driver's-side window, and Kenzie screamed as she simultaneously crawled toward the passenger side. She yelled again and scrambled for the gun in her purse before she realized it was the wild eyes and dirty face of a homeless man.

"For fuck's sake!" she yelled. "Get off my car."

The man laughed hysterically as he pointed a finger at her and then walked away.

"Damn it." Though she knew she was safe, Kenzie's hands shook as she turned the key in the ignition and threw the car in reverse. Why did men get so much pleasure from horrifying unsuspecting women? The memory of a demon sliding his knife over her flesh flashed through her mind. She bit her bottom lip as she pushed the memory away.

Shaking her head, she exited the parking garage, adrenaline still pumping through her veins. She'd never grow accustomed to some aspects of city life. Instead of heading toward the bars, she headed home. She needed some extra rest tonight to prepare for the company-wide meeting tomorrow.

Kenzie swung her car into the parking lot outside her apartment building ten minutes later. She still couldn't shake the feeling of being watched, the paranoia invading her thoughts with every movement of shadow.

Thankfully, the area was fairly well lit at night, and she'd left a light on in her apartment before leaving this morning. She shut her apartment door behind her and leaned against it for a moment. Kenzie took a few breaths to calm her nerves. She'd wrestled with anxiety since her sophomore year of college. Kenzie knew her fears were irrational but gave herself the grace to feel and work through the emotions. She wished she was still the badass girl with no fear that she used to be, but life had broken her a little. Maybe a lot.

Though she was safely in her apartment with the door locked, she couldn't shake the eerie feeling that'd come over her. Something felt off. Kenzie slipped off her heels and carried them toward the bedroom. As she stepped into the small hallway, her stomach dropped. The light in her bedroom was on. She knew she hadn't left it on because she'd never turned it on in the first place this morning. Kenzie knew she'd gotten dressed by the light of her bedside lamp. She gulped and padded back to the living room, where she'd left her purse. She reached inside and wrapped her hand over her gun.

Kenzie made her way slowly toward her bedroom, swinging the gun at every dark corner until she stepped into the room. "Who's in here?" she asked in a voice that was too shaky for her liking. Did she really think someone was going to answer back?

Kenzie checked the closet, under the bed, behind curtains, and in the bathroom before she let out a sigh of relief. Maybe she had turned it on for a moment and then ran out absentmindedly before turning it off again. She'd been almost late leaving this morning. It was possible... wasn't it? She just wasn't sure, and that didn't sit well with her.

Kenzie placed the gun on her dresser and looked at herself in the mirror. She was getting some of her own dark circles under her eyes from working too hard, but with the merger happening, she didn't see that changing anytime soon. She pulled her hair up and twisted it behind her head, clipping it in place with a claw clip from the top of her cluttered dresser.

After she changed into a t-shirt and joggers and made herself a sandwich, she settled into her favorite chair to lose herself in television. It was nights like this that she wished she still had a roommate. Kenzie liked her space and loved living alone otherwise, but the apartment was too quiet and empty.

The noise and distraction from the television did little to curb her anxiety. She turned it off and bumped up her thermostat. She rubbed her hands against her arms and stepped to the window to look down on the street below. Kenzie didn't know what possessed her to look out the window. The street was quiet at this hour on a Tuesday night, but a dark car parked on the street caught her eye. It was an antique, a 1972 Lamborghini Miura—and she'd only known one person to own one.

Travis.

It was blue, too, like the one that'd sat under a cover in his barn.

Kenzie's hand went to her mouth. She felt light-headed, and she grabbed the windowsill to steady herself. As she watched, the car's headlights came on, and it eased out on the road and drove past her apartment. Tears pricked her eyes, and she blinked them away. Now, with so much added work stress, was not the time to see dead people.

What were the odds that someone in this city had that exact car, though? Kenzie could hear her dad telling her at the car show where they'd seen one on display that only ten were built for the U.S. That was years ago. There were probably fewer around now. That's what made the car such a collector's item and why she'd been so surprised that Travis' family owned one of them. It was worth millions now.

Kenzie whimpered. It couldn't be Travis. Travis was dead. She went to his funeral and stood in the graveyard in front of the Weber family mausoleum, completely alone, with Justin somewhere at her back as she wondered if, or when, he was going to kill her for knowing too much about that night. She'd even been too scared to tell Lena about her fling with Travis or that the man she was falling in love with had been murdered. Giving Lena even that much information seemed too dangerous. She'd suffered the loss of him in silence.

She and Lena had grown apart that last half a year before Lena graduated. It wasn't hard for Kenzie to leave and start a new life at that point.

Kenzie had known turning Justin into the police would have been ludicrous. With no body and the mansion burned to nothing by ash, there was no evidence. He was rich, and his family was influential.

Could Travis have gotten away?

She'd always felt a lack of closure about Travis' death, but that was normal in grieving when there was no body to bury. She couldn't allow her mind to make up impossibilities out of hope.

Kenzie had so many nightmares about that night. A recurring one was that she attacked Justin instead of running away like a coward—and he shot her in the stomach. And as she hung there, dying in his embrace, he laughed at her stupidity before she'd wake up in a cold sweat, crying into her pillow.

Kenzie took a ragged breath, and the huff of exhalation fogged up the window. She realized someone had drawn a heart on the glass. Kenzie frowned. Surely, she'd cleaned the windows in the couple of years that she'd had this apartment.

Mark had never come to her apartment, so it couldn't have been him.

It doesn't mean anything, Kenzie.

She realized she was gripping the windowsill so tightly that her fingers were aching.

CHAPTER 25

Kenzie and Sonja walked side-by-side toward the conference room on the third floor of their building. Management would inform them about the merger today, and anxiety flooded Kenzie's system. She was sweating despite the chill in the office this morning, and she had to struggle to keep her coffee cup steady in her hand.

"You okay, sis?" Sonja asked.

"Yeah. I didn't sleep well last night." They turned into the conference room, which was standing-room only by this point.

A woman in a sharp red suit, complete with black Louboutin pumps and pouty red lips, surveyed the crowd as the rest of the employees gathered in the room. Everyone was much quieter than usual. The light banter was absent in the face of so much uncertainty. Their boss, Mr. Herschinger, stood to the side and turned on the screen where the name of the company appeared on the screen that the lady was representing.

Greyer Tech.

Kenzie pulled in a breath, and Sonja looked at her, her eyebrows knit together. Kenzie stared at the name as if the letters would give her some insight into whether this was the same Greyer family she knew from her past.

It couldn't be. Justin's father was in the aerospace sector. Publishing was far removed from that. Even in a conglomerate merger, those two types of businesses wouldn't have complementary assets.

"This is Ms. Ivy Baker, PR representative for Greyer Tech. You'll meet other members of their team eventually, but she's here today to talk about their acquisition of Dillon Books. So I'll hand it over to you, Ms. Baker," Mr. Herschinger said.

"Good morning," the woman said. "We at Greyer Tech are excited to reach out to the family at Dillon Books—and that's how Mr. Herschinger has described you—to welcome you and to assure you that this M&A will be as painless as possible and equally advantageous to both parties. For now, we're keeping the name of the publishing company, but we have lots of ideas in store for how we can mutually use both companies to do some great things in both the tech sector and publishing sector." The woman's smile didn't reach her eyes. "We believe that combining our technology and innovation with the publishing and media portfolio of this company will result in a wider reach for both companies. Mr. Herschinger will continue to head up the company, but we'll make changes as needed to make sure that everyone is supported as the company grows."

Kenzie tuned out the rest of the spiel. She felt sick to her stomach, and she wished she hadn't drunk so much sugary coffee on an empty stomach. She needed to get back to her office to research this company. Sonja glanced her way, but all Kenzie could do was widen her eyes a bit. She wanted to be positive like Sonja was trying to be about this merger, but stamped with the Greyer name, it was tainted for her.

They were passing around folders for each person, Kenzie realized as the surrounding murmurs pulled her from her thoughts.

"You okay?" Sonja asked. "You look like someone ran over your puppy."

"Yes," Kenzie muttered as she flipped through the contents of the packet. How could she explain to Sonja her fear of the Greyer name? How could she talk to anyone about what happened when she could barely process all that had happened years ago?

Stuff it down and keep surviving, Kenzie, she told herself.

"I'll be around most of the day and can answer the questions you may have one-on-one. I prefer that to a free-for-all bombardment, so please, go back to your work, and I'll come around and talk to everyone eventually today." She tucked a dark brown lock of hair behind her ear and said, "Oh, and I do need to meet quickly with..." She looked down at a list written out on a notepad. "Jameson Kemp, Sonja Kellerman, Makenzie Cameron, Gina Ramirez, and Paul Whitlock, please stay behind. Thank you, everyone!"

"Please don't let them fire us today," Kenzie murmured to herself. She loved her apartment and didn't want to lose it. She also liked food, electricity, and running water.

Sonja squeezed her arm reassuringly. "No way are they firing some of the best this business has in-house." She gave Kenzie a wink as they took a seat at the table, following the lead of Ms. Baker and Mr. Herschinger.

The woman in red eyed each of them for a moment before she continued. "Mr. Herschinger gave us a list of some of his best employees. Of those he recommended, we chose a small team that we want to represent the publishing firm along with Mr. Herschinger at the Hallowmas Masquerade Ball in two weeks. This is a very important event for us."

Ivy Baker braced herself on her fingers against the tabletop as she leaned in.

"I'll send each of you a copy of our media kit, along with an updated version of the media kit for Dillon Publishing. Familiarize yourselves with it. I'll also send you a list of VIPs you should become knowledgeable about before the ball. Speaking to them by name and knowing some background information will go a long way with these people.

"This will be a weekend-long event at the historic Gregory Rose Hotel. And each of you will get a stipend for spending as you see fit; plus, your masquerade attire will be charged to our company account. I'll send you an email soon with those details. We know it isn't cheap to attend an event like this, and we want to take the financial burden off you so you can both work and enjoy the event." She gave them her fake smile again.

"And tickets to the ball?" Sonja asked.

"Already purchased. This is a work event, but we do want you to also have fun," she reiterated. "Consider it an added bonus for your hard work with Dillon Publishing over the past few years."

And if you fuck it up, you're done, Kenzie thought Ms. Baker wanted to say but was too diplomatic at this early stage in the acquisition to point out. The five of them thanked her for the opportunity and Mr. Herschinger for the recommendation before they filed out of the conference room.

"Hell yeah!" Sonja said when they were far enough away from the conference room. "What did I tell you? This merger is going to do big things for Dillon Books. The kind of attention we can garner representing our company at an event like the Hallowmas Masquerade Ball is going to be nuts. Do you know how much those tickets cost?"

Kenzie shook her head. All she knew was that the masquerade was a big deal each year, and it was flooded with CEOs, political leaders, and high society. It was fancier than anything she'd ever attended.

"Try $500 per ticket! I looked into it a few years ago. It's a fundraiser for scholarships for underrepresented writers and artists. It's the perfect PR opportunity for Dillon Publishing. We just didn't previously have the funds for it."

"Wow, that's great," Kenzie said.

"But you don't actually sound enthusiastic."

Sonja knew Kenzie too well. It was hard to fake enthusiasm with her. "I'm a little worried, I guess," Kenzie said in a hushed tone. They'd gotten to the door to Kenzie's office, and both women went inside before Kenzie closed the door. "This could make or break our careers here. You do realize that, right?"

Sonja gave her that motherly, empathetic smile. "Stop worrying. I'm fantastic at memorizing names and faces, and you're great at being interesting enough that random people want to talk to you. You've got that allure and mystery about you that draws people in. We're going to rock the event. And we get to dress up in fancy dresses and drink champagne. What could go wrong?"

CHAPTER 26

Kenzie searched Greyer Tech online, but what little she could find was vague at best. She hadn't spent much time digging, though, before she was swamped with tasks that kept her busy most of the day.

When Kenzie left work, she headed to Mark's house. She'd texted him after lunch. She needed an endorphin release, or she'd never sleep tonight. Mark greeted her at the door with a kiss on the cheek. "Hi, Makenzie. It's been a while." He wore only sweatpants, and the trail of hair down his abs that disappeared beneath the waistband, promising that he had what she needed.

"I know," she said, coming into his house. "I've been so busy with work." She dropped her bag beside his couch.

"Have you had anything to eat?"

"Not since lunch," she said.

"Good. I made stuffed baked potatoes if you'd like one. You can top it however you like." Mark gestured toward the kitchen, where delicious smells were coming from, and Kenzie's stomach grumbled.

"Thanks," Kenzie said. He really was a sweet guy. Warmth swept through her core as she thought about what he was hiding beneath those sweats. "What I need, though, is to come. Orgasm now, food later."

"I can handle that, too," he said as he wrapped his arms around her and pulled her close. Mark was only a few inches taller than her in her heels. He kissed her neck and earlobe as his hands pulled at the blouse tucked into her pencil skirt. He unzipped her skirt and let it drop to her feet. "Leave the heels on," he said.

As she pulled her blouse over her head, he sank to his knees and licked at her pussy. He loved eating her out. They usually started this way. It made him hard as a rock to taste her and fuck her with his tongue. When he'd lapped at her pussy for a few moments, he rose and pulled her toward the bedroom.

Kenzie shook her head. She glanced at the sheer curtains. "Fuck me right here," she said. His dick already tented his sweatpants, and she massaged it through the soft material. He was so hard for her. "Sit," she told him.

He took orders well.

Mark pulled down his pants and stepped out of them as he settled down on the couch. He fumbled with a condom as he kept his eyes on her body. His cock stood at attention, ready to impale her. "Fuck, you're gorgeous," he said as he looked over her body. "Wrap that tight pussy around my dick." He grabbed her hips, impatient to get his dick inside of her, and pulled her into his lap so that she faced the windows at the front of his house. She saw the headlights of cars traveling up and down his street through his sheer curtains, and as he eased her down onto him and filled her up, she threw her head back and her tits forward as pleasure filled her. She wondered if any of the people in their cars could see her tits bouncing up and down as he jackhammered into her like his life depended on it.

"Fuck, you feel good," he said.

"You do, too." She bounced on his cock harder. She wanted it rough tonight. Rougher than he usually gave her. "Fuck me from behind." She raised off him, knelt on the couch so that her arms rested along one couch arm, and angled her pussy up for him.

Mark slid his fingers across her clit, and she shivered. "That's a pretty pussy I'm about to fill up." Mark grabbed her ass and thrust into her just liked she loved, and he fucked her with such force that she could barely hold herself up from the assault he was giving her pussy. He rubbed her clit for a bit before he stuck his wet finger into the entrance of her asshole. "I want in there, too," he said.

This was something new, and it sent a jolt of electricity straight to her pussy. The idea of his fat dick invading her tiny asshole scared her, honestly, but just the mention of it, the idea of him railing her little, tight hole, sent her over the edge. Kenzie rode out the orgasm with a moan of satisfaction, and he stilled his movements to give her a chance to enjoy every second. He kept his finger in her asshole, which made her feel so full, and he thrust a few more times.

"Your pussy is so hot and swollen. I fucking love it," he said as he gave a grunt and came.

"What was the ass thing?" she asked.

"Just something I've been thinking about. I'm up for trying it out anytime you feel like it."

"My, my, I think you're getting more adventurous," Kenzie teased.

"You think the neighbors got an eye full?" Mark asked. He pulled off her heels as she lowered herself. He pulled her to standing, though she still felt wobbly from the orgasm. When she glanced over her shoulder with a smirk, he said, "Shower time."

He led her to his shower, turned on the water, and let it heat up while he removed his condom and stepped into the steam with her. He lathered up his loofah and washed her body as the hot water washed away the tension from the day.

By the time he was finished washing her and himself, he was hard again. Mark looked down at his dick with pride. "I can't help myself around you," he said with a smirk.

When he turned off the water, Kenzie knelt without a word and licked and sucked at his swollen cock. He tasted sweet from the Dial soap he'd used, and she took him as deep down her throat as she could while he leaned back and enjoyed the blowjob. At first, Kenzie swirled her fingers around her swollen, sensitive clit. Then, Kenzie fondled his balls with one hand and jacked him off with the other, and in another few minutes, he was coming in her mouth. Kenzie swallowed the salty, bitter cum and licked at the tip of his dick until she thought she'd gotten it all. When she looked up at him, Mark was looking lovingly down at her face.

Kenzie rose. Though she wanted to fuck him some more, she didn't like the look he was giving her. "I think

I'll take that food to go. My company is in the middle of a merger, and I need my rest." Kenzie gave him a quick peck on the lips.

Mark pouted. "I was hoping you'd stay over tonight. I wouldn't mind a few more rounds with you."

"Maybe next time," Kenzie said as she stepped out and wrapped a towel around herself. If she spent the night, Mark might catch more feelings, and she didn't want this to become complicated. She'd never spent the night before, and she felt like the invitation was a sign that he wanted more. She liked the ease of their friendship. Besides, how could she make room in her heart when so much of it was still consumed with grief?

"Dillon Books is merging with another company?"

"Yeah, really, it's a conglomerate with a tech company. Greyer Tech? Have you ever heard of it?"

Mark dried his hair with his towel. "Nope. But I don't really follow tech companies, so that's not saying much." Mark owned a chain of gyms. It's how they'd met. Kenzie went through a phase where she thought she could chase her demons away with enough sweat and muscle fatigue, but it hadn't worked very well. She'd met Mark at one of his gyms, and they'd become friends. Only recently had they begun sleeping together.

"I have a bad feeling about it," Kenzie confided.

"You aren't great with change," Mark said gently.

Kenzie wanted to be irritated with him, but he was right. "No, I guess not."

Mark tied his towel at his waist and massaged her shoulders. "It's going to be okay. You're good at your job.

They'd be stupid to let you go, but even if that happens, another publishing house will snap you up in no time. Don't worry." He kissed her damp shoulder.

Kenzie nodded. She knew it was pointless to worry. "Thanks, Mark. You always know what to say to make me feel better."

"What are friends for?" Mark's tone was light, but she thought she heard a note of regret in it.

CHAPTER 27

It's been years since I've seen her pretty doll-like face. Kenzie was the girl who got away, and I never moved past it. No woman has ever affected me that way. I'm an unfeeling, wicked monster of a man. I could cut and pick people apart or set them on fire with no remorse. Yet, before she left, I couldn't keep my mind off her. It wasn't the usual derision that I felt for other women. It wasn't a sick curiosity to see the light fade from her eyes as I choked her to death.

Oh, I'd love to get my hands around her delicate throat. I'd throttle her, but I wouldn't crush her.

This feeling I had for her was different.

I wanted to toy with her, sure, but I wanted her acceptance, too. I wanted her love and adoration, and for a time, I had it. I wanted to possess her in a way that was more intimate than I'd been capable of before her.

I tried to forget her. I hunted and killed. Yet, my mind always traveled back to her, with her cherry-red lips and her heart-shaped face. She's the love of my life. Either she'll be mine, or I'll tear her apart so no one else can have her.

I've been obsessed with Kenzie since she left. I've watched her from afar, keeping tabs on her movements online and through financial records. I'd sometimes get to see her beautiful smile on social media. I've grown my wealth over time so that one day, I might impress her and make her mine. And now that I'm ready, I'm stalking her every move.

I've only recently come into the city to get closer to her. Finding an apartment near her was easy. Watching her movements unobserved in the city was easy, too. This isn't New York, but it's not our rural little town in Tennessee, either. It's nothing for me to walk half a block down the street behind her without being seen.

I've watched her at work. I love watching how her wavy blonde hair falls across her cheek as she pours over manuscripts, a pen tapping her bottom lip—that lip I'd love to bite—as she thinks. I toyed with writing a book, one that is our story but how I see it ending, and sending it to her under a pseudonym, but my luck would be that it'd get tossed in the trash as an unsolicited manuscript, and I'd have done all that for nothing.

She's been at her lover's house tonight. I watched them for a while, until I couldn't stand to see any more of it. Until I was seething with a rage that threatened to incinerate me from within. That beefy motherfucker doesn't deserve the privilege of touching her soft skin. I can't stand the thought of his meaty hands digging into the flesh of her thighs, of tasting and relishing what I've claimed as mine. When I saw him eating her pussy, I almost lost it and burnt the whole fucking place down, with him and her in it.

I have other plans, though.

I wonder if her alabaster skin would turn into red whelps if I flailed it with a cat-o'-nine-tails. Maybe not hard enough to bring blood and scar her perfect skin, but light swats that would make her cry and beg for mercy. I want to punish her for being such a naughty girl. If I hung her up, would she melt in my hands? I fantasize about stuffing a bullet up her ass and turning it on while simultaneously teasing her clit with a vibrator and making her sob from so many orgasms. My mind wanders to so many delightful things I want to do to her, but until I get my hands on Kenzie, I'll entertain my fantasies another way.

I rolled aside the bookshelf hiding the door to the dressing room that I've sound-proofed and converted into a playroom over the past few weeks, complete with a sex swing with metal loops for cuffs, various floggers and crops, and a cage for containing the animal until I'm ready to use her. As soon as I opened the door, the sweet sound of whimpering reached my ears, and it set my dick to twitching. I can smell her sex in the air. I ravaged her pussy last night and left it filled and dripping with my cum.

I dragged the woman out of the puppy kennel by the hair of her head to take out my annoyance with seeing Kenzie fucking Loverboy. If Kenzie hadn't put on such a licentious show, this woman might have lived another day.

The woman, who was easily thirty but stood cowering before me like a little girl, had an ugly c-section scar across her bare stomach, but otherwise, she had a nice body. She'd followed me like a puppy when I flashed money before her eyes two days ago. I'd taken her clothes when I got her into the apartment. She'd thought it was a harmless sex game.

"You like kinky sex?" I'd asked her, taking my belt off and readying it for her first beating.

She'd nodded, her eyes heavy with desire. When I'd unbuttoned and took off my shirt, she licked her lips as she eyed the tattoos across my back and chest. Of course she did. She was ready for it. These 30-something housewives were all bored with fucking their husbands and taking care of children, decade after decade. They'd try anything once just to break the tedium of their lives.

I wondered now if she was still dwelling on the monotony of her life.

"Get in the swing, my pet. We're going to have some more fun tonight."

It wouldn't matter. I needed to destroy something. After I pounded her asshole until she screamed for mercy, I planned on slitting her throat and fucking her mouth until the blood pooling there grew cold—or I got off again—whichever came first. Then, I'd clean myself up, cut her into pieces, wrap them all in plastic, shove the parts of her body into luggage, and put the luggage into the back of the stolen car I'd parked in the alley a few hours ago. I had the perfect place to dump the car, cover it with gasoline, and set it on fire.

And if by tomorrow morning, I haven't satiated the rage with all that destruction, I'll go to that fucking Mark's house, chop his dick off, and feed it to him for breakfast before I bludgeon him to death.

CHAPTER 28

When Kenzie got home from Mark's, she stepped out of her heels at the door. She hung her purse and keyring on the hook behind the front door and went to the kitchen with the container he'd put her stuffed baked potato into before sending her home to rest.

She peeled off the plastic top and inhaled deeply. Damn, the man could cook. The potato, which was still warm, was topped with grilled chicken, crispy bacon, Swiss cheese, sour cream, and just the right amount of diced green onions—enough to give it a zing of flavor but not overpower the other ingredients.

Kenzie unzipped the tight skirt she'd worn to work and tossed it on the end of her couch before returning to her food. She pulled a fork from the drawer and dug in. Sex always made her ravenous, and she'd been hungry before she stopped at Mark's. It was already past 8.

"Mmm," she said aloud as she chewed the first bite. Her eyes rolled back in her head. How could a freaking potato be so good? Kenzie sat down cross-legged on the couch to devour her supper. After eating a few more bites, she returned to the kitchen and grabbed a glass from the cabinet, but something made her pause. She couldn't put her finger on it, but something seemed different. Off. She eyed her canisters that held sugar, creamer, cereal, and pasta. She touched one of them with the tip of her finger. They were perfectly spaced, one finger-width between each. She narrowed her eyes. Kenzie was a haphazard woman. What were the chances that in her haste to make a cup of coffee that morning, she'd put the canisters back just so?

Kenzie's eyes swung toward the door. No signs of forced entry. "Get a grip," she chided herself. No one was going to break in and rearrange her canisters, for crying out loud. She shook her head and poured herself a glass of tea before returning to her meal. When she was finally full, she pulled open her laptop to check her work emails. An email had come through with directions on which boutiques Greyer Tech had charge accounts with so that they could rent their attire for the masquerade.

Kenzie looked up the venue. She was meticulous and over-prepared with work. The article read:

Each year, during the first week of November, the beautiful Gregory Rose Hotel hosts the Hallowmas Masquerade Ball. French architect Baptiste Tremblay designed the ballroom in 1902. With over 6,400 square feet in an L-shaped design, complete with a stage at one end, the ballroom has been home to various and sundry galas, parties, conventions, concerts, fundraisers, and dances over its more than century-long history. It features floor-to-ceiling windows that look out upon the lights of the city at night and blue skies during the day. It also features original wood floors, varnished to a glass-like gleam, and gilded 30-foot ceilings. Dancing across the ballroom transports partygoers to a palatial room in a faraway fairy kingdom rather than a historic hotel in our fair city.

Okay, Kenzie thought. *I guess it's worth getting a little excited about.*

The article described the fundraising efforts of the ball and famous patrons of the arts who'd attended recent balls in the past.

She scrolled through images of women in exquisite ball gowns, their masquerade masks removed for photos.

Kenzie imagined herself gliding across the floor of the ballroom in the arms of a masked man.

She picked up her phone and texted Sonja.

> Shit, do you know how to ballroom dance?

It took Sonja about twenty minutes to get back to her.

> I haven't waltzed in years. I just signed us up for two classes.

> One will be tomorrow night, and the other will be Tuesday. 2 hours each! Waltz, Foxtrot, and Tango. We'll be ready!

> If you say so...

CHAPTER 29

The next day, Kenzie worked until lunch. Mr. Herschinger advised them to take the afternoon to search for attire for the ball. Sonja and Kenzie went together to one place that Ms. Baker's email listed as a boutique with a Greyer Tech charge account.

When the sales associate heard the words 'Greyer Tech charge account' come out of Sonja's mouth, she was falling over herself to help them find dresses. For a moment, she flitted away, so Kenzie took the opportunity to see what Sonja knew about the company.

"Have you heard anything about this Greyer Tech? What do they do? Who runs it? Their website was so vague," Kenzie said as she moved aside dresses she didn't find interesting. She wanted something alluring but also something that she could move around in. The event wouldn't be fun if she couldn't enjoy herself.

"Not much. Just that it's a tech firm out of Nashville, I think? It was started by some kid right out of college. You know, basically how they all start—Apple, Meta, Microsoft, and the other tech conglomerates. My advice is to buy stock shares now," Sonja said with a grin. "If they're already buying up other companies, they're forging ahead, not falling behind." She held up a royal blue dress with lots of tulle on the skirt and sequins that curved around the bodice. "What about this one?"

"I like the color, but it's a little floofy."

"No, it's a lot floofy." Sonja stuck it back on the rack. "I want some floof, but not so much that I can't cozy up to some hunky, single CEO."

"I'm just wondering because I was involved with a Greyer back in high school. Justin Reese Greyer? I have no idea what he did with his life, though. I lost touch." *On purpose.*

Sonja shrugged. "Doesn't ring a bell. Oh, look at this one! It would look great on you." It was a gold satin sheath dress, but what was interesting about it was that half of the skirt was floor-length satin gathered on one hip, while the other side of the skirt was a see-through material with ornate gold lace swirling across it and a short skirt beneath that hit only about mid-thigh so that one leg was visible. The top was covered in the same lace detail, with off-the-shoulder straps covered in gold lace.

"Wow! That's gorgeous." Kenzie grabbed it from Sonja to try on. She also pulled a plain purple satin strapless ballgown with lots of gathering at the waist and an interesting bustline detail. "Found anything yet?" When Sonja held up a black gown studded with rhinestone across the taffeta bottom and a corset top with black lace details, Kenzie raised her eyebrows. "Considerably less floofy—and beautiful, too. It looks like a starry sky. Okay, let's go try these on."

Kenzie tried the satin purple dress on first. It was her favorite color, after all. Though it was pretty and fit her well, it didn't seem dressy enough for this affair. She didn't have expensive jewelry to dress up an understated gown like this, though she supposed she could find some costume jewelry that would suffice.

She removed that one and put the gold one on. When she turned toward the mirror, she gasped. It was that gorgeous and worth an audible gasp. Hugging her in all the right places, it was sultry but also demure, making her look like a million bucks.

"Oh, Makenzie," she heard Sonja say from the next dressing room over. "This black dress is it!"

Kenzie said, "I think I've found mine, too. Step out, and let's see."

As both women exited their dressing rooms, they erupted with squeals at each other's dresses. An onlooker would have thought they were high schoolers buying dresses for their first prom. Kenzie laughed at the thought. As Sonja twirled, the starry sky of her skirt streaked and blurred. "Yes, that dress suits you," Kenzie said. "That's the one."

"Okay, I love my dress, but I'm slightly jealous of you in that one. I mean, I couldn't fill it out like that, but by all means, you go your sweet ass to the ball looking like a gilded goddess and knock 'em dead."

"I'm afraid the gold of this one is going to wash me out, especially with my blonde hair."

"That's an easy fix. We'll go to the salon this weekend, and you can get some caramel or honey lowlights added in to warm up your color. It won't be a drastic change, but it'll be enough of a difference that the deep gold color of your dress will look amazing on you." Sonja hooked her arm with Kenzie's, and they both turned toward the mirrors. They were stunning.

Kenzie nodded, truly excited for the first time about this event, her apprehension about the company merger only a nagging worry in the back of her mind. The women finished up their shopping by finding the perfect shoes and masquerade masks to polish off their looks for the special night.

***

Kenzie went home to change out of her work outfit and shoes before Sonja picked her up for ballroom dancing lessons. Kenzie and Sonja grabbed wraps to eat after work on the ride over to the dance studio and discussed their hair and makeup for the night.

They tripped and stomped their way through the first ballroom dance class. They'd been paired up with two male dancers who were also learners, though they had more experience than the two women. Kenzie stepped on the toe of her poor partner at least five times before the lesson was over. She vowed to spend the weekend watching online tutorials and practicing when Sonja dropped her off at her apartment. There was no way she wanted that to happen at the ball. What if someone really important asked her to dance?

It was already past 9 when she arrived home again, and her legs hurt. She wanted to soak in a hot bath and sleep.

Kenzie pulled up her hair into a claw clip and was about to get undressed when she heard a knock at her door.

A plainclothes detective stood on the threshold of her apartment, his badge, which he held up to her in his hand, the only indication that he was a cop. "Makenzie Cameron?" he asked.

She nodded.

"I'm Detective Lincoln. Do you know Mark Flores?"

"Yes, he's a friend of mine. Why? Is he in trouble?" She furrowed her brows. She couldn't imagine what kind of trouble he could have gotten into. He was about as straight-laced as they came.

"Just a friend?"

Kenzie's brow furrowed. "What's this about? Why are you asking me about Mark?"

"May I come in, Ms. Cameron?"

"Um, yes." She pulled open the door wider, and the detective stepped into her apartment, sweeping the place with his eyes before allowing them to land back on her face.

"Why would you think he might be in trouble?" he asked with an emotionless face.

"Because an officer comes to my door asking me if I know him. That usually signals that something's wrong," she said, her voice unwavering, though her heart beat a mile a minute.

"What's your relationship with Mr. Flores?"

"I told you. We're friends."

"Ms. Cameron, it seems like you might not know, so I'm sorry to be the one to tell you, but are you aware that Mark Flores was killed?"

"What?" Her heart dropped. Why? How? So many questions flooded her mind, but nothing else would come out of her mouth, though her jaw worked up and down as if trying to form more questions.

"Would you like a seat?" He motioned toward her couch.

"Yes," she said, one hand going to the back of her neck. She sat but fidgeted with the hem of the kimono she wore over her camisole. "He's dead? But I just saw him last night."

The detective nodded. "It was very violent. Neighbors said that you sometimes came over to his house for visits."

There was no point in lying to the detective to save her embarrassment. If he caught her in a lie, it would only make her look guilty.

"Yes, Mark and I had a physical relationship. But it wasn't emotional. I mean, we weren't dating. I cared about him." She pursed her lips but forged forward. "We were friends who sometimes slept together."

"One of his neighbors said he witnessed you having sexual relations with Mark the night of the murder. Through the living room window."

Kenzie's cheeks burned with the heat of embarrassment. She raised her chin. "Yes, Wednesday night, I'd gone over. He sent me home with food. I still have his container," she said stupidly, as if that mattered anymore. She shut her eyes. When she opened them, the detective was watching her. "Did the Peeping Tom also see who killed Mark?" Saying it aloud made her sick to her stomach. She wanted to cry, but she would not do it in front of the stranger.

Without answering her, Detective Lincoln asked, "Do you do that with other men? Have 'physical relationships' as you call it?"

The way he said it sounded judgmental. "How is that relevant?" she snapped.

"I'm trying to establish a motive. If you only considered it sex, but Mark thought it was something else, he might have gotten into an altercation with another of your lovers."

"He's the only one," she whispered. She cleared her throat. "I'm not sleeping with anyone else."

"You sure about that?"

"Yes!" For fuck's sake. Why wouldn't he let it rest? Maybe she wasn't the most chaste woman in the city, but he acted like she was a harlot.

"I only ask because a neighbor of yours said that she's seen a man leaving your apartment late at night a couple of times over the past few weeks."

"What? Either she's lying or... or someone's been in my apartment without my knowledge. Because I haven't had *any* men in this apartment. Not since my dad helped me move in." She frowned. "Do you think I'm in danger, too? What if whoever killed Mark has been here and plans to do the same to me?"

"I'm not sure, but it wouldn't be a bad idea to maybe buy a door cam or something in the meantime."

Kenzie snorted with derision. "What good will that do? Besides giving you an image of a killer after the fact."

"Much of the time, a victim knows their killer. Maybe you could recognize the person who may have been in your apartment. Have you had any other suspicions that someone might have been in your home without your knowledge?"

She thought of the canisters on her counter neatly ordered and the heart she'd found drawn on the window. But those things sounded silly and borderline paranoid, so she didn't mention them. She shook her head.

"You can always call 9-1-1 if you feel your life is in danger. If you suspect anyone is here, get out of the apartment and call us. Had you gotten into any arguments with Mark Flores recently?" he asked.

"No, Mark and I were great. He was a good guy." She shrugged.

"Where were you early the following morning?" he asked.

"Here, sleeping or getting up and ready for work, depending on how early you're talking."

"Time of death was approximately 3 a.m., early enough that no one saw anyone suspicious going into or coming out of the home after you left." The detective stood. "Thank you for answering my questions."

"You're welcome. I sincerely hope you catch the bastard who did this, not only for my own peace of mind but also for Mark. He didn't deserve to die a gruesome death." He had so many plans for his future. Now, none of them would happen, and it infuriated her.

Detective Lincoln nodded and turned toward the door but stopped before going out. "You're not leaving the state anytime soon, are you, Ms. Cameron?"

"No, no traveling plans."

"Okay, I'll be in touch if I have any more questions for you."

CHAPTER 30

Kenzie couldn't believe how quickly the night of the masquerade came. She'd left work early to pick up her mask, eat, and get ready for the event.

She hadn't heard another word from Detective Lincoln, so she assumed they were no closer to finding Mark's killer than the day he'd questioned her. His death was weighing heavily on her mind as she got ready.

Kenzie curled her hair, and it looked amazing with the new lowlights Sonja talked her into getting. Her makeup looked good, and she felt confident. She spritzed on her favorite perfume before putting on her ball gown.

A limo service would pick her up any minute. Greyer Tech and Dillon Books wanted to arrive at the event together to convey a connected front for the media. The six from Dillon Books, plus three from Greyer Tech, would be in attendance. Kenzie was surprised that so few from Greyer Tech were coming to the event, but she guessed they probably attended this event every year and didn't need the publicity as much as Dillon Books did.

Kenzie looked at her dress in the mirror and pulled the mask from the box where she'd kept it since purchasing it. A note fluttered out and onto the floor. Was it a receipt from the shop where she bought it? The simple piece of white paper was folded in half. She opened it. Written in meticulous cursive was a familiar quote:

"No use resisting... abandon thought and let the dream descend! What raging fire shall flood the soul? What rich desires unlock its door? What sweet seductions lie before us?"

Kenzie frowned. She knew the quote, but where was it from? She'd read so many books in college and many more since then. Or was it the lyrics from a song she knew? And was this the little touch of personalization so many boutiques were now adding to purchases? She wondered if this was something the shop put into all their mask boxes. It certainly fit. She didn't have time to ponder it. She placed the note back into the box and lifted the mask to her face.

Kenzie turned back to the mirror. She covered half her face with the white owl-like mask with gold foil accents. She set the mask in place with pins and smiled. It was beautiful. She'd always found masks intriguing, and this one made her feel mysterious and alluring.

Sonja dinged her phone with a message to tell her that the limo was almost to her apartment. Kenzie grabbed the little clutch she was taking with her keys, some lipstick, and some cash, and she locked up and ran downstairs to wait for the car to arrive. It pulled up, long and sleek beside her on the street, and someone from inside swung open one door near the back of the car.

A gentleman in a dark blue tux with a navy blue and cyan mask climbed out and held out his hand to help her maneuver into the car, which wasn't an easy task in the dress and five-inch heels.

"Thank you." She thought it was Jameson from the office, but she wasn't sure. It was amazing how much of an identity a mask could conceal. She realized how heavily she relied on face recognition when she couldn't see the person.

"You look stunning," Jameson said before he climbed back into the limo.

"Makenzie, I love that dress," Ivy Baker said as Kenzie took a seat between her and Sonja. "Good choice." Ivy was wearing her customary red but in a mermaid-style satin with a sweetheart neckline encrusted with crystals. She wore a minimal red mask, the kind that barely covered her eyes and left no questions about who she was. Kenzie figured she was the kind of woman who would want to be instantly recognized.

"Thank you." She smoothed the gold fabric with her hand and placed her clutch in her lap.

As the car moved, Ivy pointed out the rest of the people in the limo. "The man beside Mr. Herschinger in the red fox mask is Dante, top-level management at Greyer Tech, and Billy, in the green and yellow mask, is our best software engineer. One more stop to pick up Gina Ramirez, and then we're headed to the hotel. Do you feel confident in networking with the VIPs tonight?"

The men in the car already had their heads bent toward each other in their own conversations, and music played lightly in the background.

"Sure," Kenzie said. "This is a great opportunity for Dillon Books. I appreciate being included. And dressing up was fun."

Sonja leaned in. "Makenzie is a pro at events like these. She may seem quiet, but the men flock to her. She'll have no trouble getting everyone's attention, especially in that dress."

Ivy handed a glass of champagne to Kenzie and topped her own off. "Cheers to that!"

Sonja held up her champagne flute, and the three of them clinked their glasses together. "To Dillon Books and Greyer Tech!"

Kenzie smiled. "Cheers!"

CHAPTER 31

People from the media and arriving attendees filled the steps into the venue, pausing for pictures or quick interviews. The nine of them stopped only for a picture before entering the old hotel. In the lobby, it was less crowded, and Kenzie could breathe easier. Mr. Herschinger, the men from Greyer Tech, and Maria stayed in the lobby to talk to people they knew. The three women, plus Jameson, grabbed an elevator and took it up to the top floor to the ballroom, which was grander than even pictures, and the article description could do it justice. The gold gleamed like old money, and the floors shone so brightly under the chandeliers overhead that it was disorienting, like a dream.

Upon entering the doors to the ballroom, they came into the smaller part of the L-shaped room where an open bar and most of the tables were set up, each with ten chairs and a beautiful centerpiece of white roses, greenery, gold accents, and candles. The dance floor was the long part of the L, and Kenzie saw a small stage at the far end. She wondered if they'd have a band playing for the music.

Kenzie plucked a champagne flute off a waiting tray. Her buzz from the champagne in the limo was long gone.

"Don't sit until your feet are aching," Ivy said, grabbing a champagne flute for herself. "Take every opportunity you have to rub elbows with the other partygoers tonight. It'll make tomorrow's events more interesting."

Kenzie realized they hadn't been told what they'd be doing for the rest of the event. "What's on the agenda for tomorrow?"

"A luncheon, drinks, and a play tomorrow night. We'll talk about it later. I see the senator. Let's go say 'hello,'" she said as she led the way to five men in black tuxes gathered near the dance floor.

Kenzie recognized the shortest as the senator she'd memorized from her PR packet. He was currently working on a labor bill to protect employee's rights.

All five men turned as the trio of women approached them. They were pleasant enough, but Kenzie allowed the others to engage in conversation while she surveyed the party-goers entering the venue. Politics wasn't her favorite topic.

Kenzie had to admit that the beginning of the event was boring, other than seeing a famous actor or a politician who wanted to chat with her. She tried to highlight Dillon Books whenever she could, but she didn't know enough about Greyer Tech to discuss the merger. Kenzie tried to keep Sonja close so that Sonja could do most of the talking for them—she lived for it—but she'd been snatched by Ivy to meet another of Greyer Tech's employees who'd shown up on his own while the mayor and his wife, who was on the library association board, held Kenzie captive in a conversation about recent book trends. The topic was easy for her, so she could have chatted with them all night about books.

Now, she was trying to pay attention to an older gentleman telling her about the problem with the current state of the energy crisis, when the first deep, resonating note of a stringed instrument snapped her attention to the small stage at the far end of the ballroom. In the quartet, she spotted two violinists, a violist, and a cellist. All of them were men in black tuxes and matching full-face Venetian masks covered in jewels.

"Ah, look at that. Time to dance," the older gentleman said with a smile. "Would you do me the honor?"

She nodded and took his outstretched hand. Anything to not have to hear more about the energy crisis. "If I didn't know better, I'd think you were holding me enthralled in conversation, waiting for the quartet to start playing," she teased.

He laughed. "I like it when a woman understands a man's true intentions." They waltzed, and the gentleman was a good lead. He smoothly guided her across the dance floor as others joined in. "Besides, it does my pride good to say that I got the first dance with the most beautiful woman here."

"And how would you know that?" she asked. "Half my face is covered by a mask."

"When you're as old as I am, you can pick out beautiful women even in the dark," he said with a wink. He had a mischievous grin that made her comfortable despite his flirting. "You know, dear," he continued, moving closer to her ear so he could drop his voice, "I think you'd be the perfect newest addition to a private party we're having downstairs later. If you don't mind—ahem—lots of partners."

Kenzie's eyes widened. Was he inviting her to an orgy? "That is, um, interesting, but—"

The song ended, and another man tapped her shoulder, saving her from having to let the older gentleman down. "May I cut in?"

This man was much younger, though she couldn't tell much else about him. He wore a full mask of black with gold accents, which matched his tux. His vest and tie were the same hue of gold as her dress. The older man handed her off, and she stepped toward the younger gentleman. He took her firmly in his arms and waltzed.

The quartet played a mixture of classical and modern songs, which Kenzie enjoyed. Right now, they were playing a beautiful Bach concerto she sometimes listened to while she worked at night. The stringed instruments had become her favorite after Travis played the cello for her. They calmed her mind when nothing else would. Tonight, the music reminded her of him, and it left her feeling wistful and melancholic.

Kenzie looked up at her dance partner. "We match a little. Don't you think?" she asked to break the ice.

"We do," he said. "Your mask is nicer than mine, though."

"Going for the dark and mysterious look tonight?" Kenzie asked.

"Being anonymous has its advantages," he said. "You dance well." He watched her with dark eyes.

"You're being nice. I'm terrible at this, but I'm trying." She smiled. She wished she could see at least half his face. The unchanging face of the mask made her nervous. She couldn't tell if the man smiled at her comment or smirked at her inadequacy. Because they were dancing, she couldn't read his body language. She only had the pressure of his hand in hers and at her back. "You, on the other hand, lead very smoothly. You make my job easy." She noticed that his cologne, though faint, was spicy and enticing. Expensive.

"Years of cotillion," he said.

"Ah, that explains it. I never introduced myself. I'm Makenzie Cameron, an editor at Dillon Books. You are?"

"Your new boss."

Kenzie missed a step as she leaned back, as if she might now see through the mask. "Really?"

He guided her easily through the misstep. "I own Greyer Tech."

"Oh, well, nice to meet you. I'm looking forward to getting to know everyone as the companies merge."

"Likewise," he said.

He seemed to be a man of few words. Maybe he simply wished she'd shut up so he could enjoy the dance.

"Just avoid the orgy on floor six, and you'll be fine."

Kenzie's cheeks warmed, and she was glad that the mask hid most of the flush that spread over her skin. Kenzie pursed her lips and concentrated on avoiding his toes. It was easier than looking into his eyes.

Suddenly, the song ended, and they parted. Someone else asked her to dance, and Kenzie bent her head toward her new boss. "Thanks for the dance, Mr..." Instead of answering her, he turned away.

Kenzie danced with a few other men before taking a break to find a drink. As she walked toward the tables and bar area, the musicians played "Creep," and it stopped her in her tracks. She turned to face the quartet, but she was far enough away that she couldn't make out anything distinguishable about any of them. Her eyes scanned over the cellist. The only difference from the other men playing was dark tattoos creeping down his hands from the cuffs of his tux.

Travis hadn't had tattoos.

"It's not Travis," she whispered and turned away. It was only a coincidence.

There were so many people in the ballroom now that it was getting stuffy. She grabbed a champagne flute and drank half of it before heading toward the tables.

God, she missed him. Especially surrounded by masked men. Mostly, she felt the ache of what might have been. It's true that she hadn't known Travis long, but she'd felt closer and more intimate with him than with any man before or since. Life hadn't been quite the same after him. She went through the motions and carried on because she had to, but it was all so dull, like living in black and white after she'd seen color.

Kenzie spied a vacant seat at a table and sat. She felt dizzy and lightheaded. If she didn't slow down on the alcohol, she'd end up making an ass of herself tonight.

Her eyes fell on the quartet again as dancers parted the crowd on the dance floor, and she watched as the cellist moved his bow across the strings while his fingers hammered the strings of the neck. The four of them played beautifully together.

The song ended, and the quartet paused for a few beats as they prepared for the next song. Kenzie pulled off her mask and fanned her face with it. As Kenzie raised her glass to her lips again, the music began, and she sat her flute down so hard on the table that it was a wonder she didn't break the stem. It was the song Travis had played from "The Phantom of the Opera."

Her heart stuttered. Her breaths came ragged as she watched the cellist move his bow across the string, each sad note pulling at her heartstrings.

Kenzie wanted to stand up, run to him, and fling his mask from his face to demand why he was playing Travis' songs and torturing her poor, hurt soul.

Was this now too much of a coincidence, or was she losing her damn mind? A tear escaped down her cheek, and she quickly brushed it away.

"Tired of dancing and networking already?"

Kenzie looked up toward the voice. The man in the black and gold mask stood beside her.

Ivy's comment about taking every opportunity she had to network rang in her mind. Was her new boss annoyed she was sitting? The stupid mask he wore remained emotionless. "A little. I got hot and thirsty dancing." She held up her champagne flute.

He leaned his head to the right as if he was trying to figure something out.

The gesture made her nervous. All she could see was the sparkle of his eyes, which were in shadow beyond the mask.

"And the tear?"

Kenzie raised one shoulder in a shrug. She couldn't explain to her boss that she thought her dead lover was playing her a song.

"No one's hit on you, have they?" His voice had changed. There was an edge of menace to it.

"Beyond an orgy invitation?" she said with a laugh, but he only tightened his grip on her chair. "No, nothing like that." Kenzie gave him a weak smile, the only thing she could muster to reassure him. "I just needed a breather." She placed her mask back on her face.

The music stopped as the quartet took a set break.

He leaned down so that his mask was near her ear. "I hate these events. Ivy makes me come because they're good for PR." He held out a hand. "I know a place where you can cool off and escape some of the incessant boasting and complaining—and being constantly handled by men. Come with me."

CHAPTER 32

Kenzie took his hand and followed him through the crowd of people toward the stage at the end of the ballroom.

As they passed through a door, she bumped into one of the masked quartet players. "Oh, excuse me." The masked musician grabbed her as if to steady her. "No, I'm fine," she said as she looked down at the hands on her arms. Tattoos. The cellist. "Thank you," she said as she untangled herself from his embrace.

Kenzie turned, caught up with her boss, and climbed a narrow stairway that led to a door. He pulled out a key from his pocket and unlocked it. He and Kenzie stepped out onto the roof of the hotel. She heard the music resume below them in the ballroom, but it was only a faint sound up here. The door closed behind her, and the cool air kissed her flushed skin.

"This is nice," Kenzie said. "I didn't realize how hot I'd gotten inside." She pulled off her mask. "I'm sorry. I didn't catch your name downstairs. I'm terribly embarrassed that I don't yet know who my boss is."

The man reached up to pull off his mask and hesitated.

Kenzie stared expectantly at him. Why would he hesitate?

"Kenzie," he said, "I want you to understand that this is a surprise to me, too."

"I don't understand." Kenzie frowned. No one around here called her that. No one had called her that since college back home.

He removed the mask.

Kenzie's face fell. "Justin! How—"

Justin held up his free hand. "I didn't know you lived in the city, let alone worked for the company I wanted to acquire."

Her pulse quickened as her brain caught up. This was the person who killed the man she loved. And he was her boss now? How fucked up was Fate to put her in this position?

She'd been the only witness. No one else knew what she knew. She hadn't even told Lena. She'd been too afraid to put her friend in danger.

Fear rose inside her. She was on top of a tall building alone with him. If he killed her, no one would even hear her scream. Was she still at risk of his wrath after all these years? Or was it only a sour memory for him? A blip on his way up? It was a night forever burned in her memory, a night that changed the course of her life, but that didn't mean that it had been so significant to him. "Why are we up here, Justin?"

"Ivy told me a Makenzie was at the event from Dillon Books, but I didn't put two and two together because you always went by Kenzie in college."

Kenzie backed away from him a few steps.

"When I realized it was you, I was floored. I needed to talk to you alone. There are too many people down there."

Kenzie took another step back. Too many people to see him hurt her?

"Please let me explain. You never gave me that chance before. You avoided me at all costs after that night," Justin said.

So that night was still on his conscience. Kenzie nodded once to give him the incentive to continue. The alternative was that he could throw her from the rooftop. She had enough champagne in her system that it could look like an accident. So, for now, she'd listen.

"Travis was unhinged. I know you couldn't see that back then, but he was manipulating you—and killing people, like the maniac that he was. I shot him, and then, I ran after you—not to hurt you but to tell you why I did it. He would've hurt other people. He was eventually going to hurt you, too.

"When I couldn't find you, I went back to the house. Travis had gotten up, and we fought. I hit him hard—so hard that I thought I'd killed him or that the loss of blood had." Justin sighed deeply as if the rest was hard to tell her. He looked skyward, searching for words. "He slumped into a heap on the front porch. Then, I dragged him into the house, went back to my truck, grabbed my gasoline can, and lit the place on fire. I was terrified that with his influence over you, I'd go down for crimes *he* committed, and you'd back up his story."

Someone banged on the door to the stairwell behind them. Kenzie barely paid it any attention, though, because something from Justin's account of that night didn't ring true, and her heart thundered in her chest at the inconsistency.

Two gunshots.

Kenzie narrowed her eyes. "You're not telling me the truth. I know you're not. There was a second shot that night. Either you shot him a second time, or you shot at me. I remember it because I was fucking terrified for my life—and for his. But either way, your story isn't accurate."

Justin clenched his jaw. "No, I just forgot about the second shot. He came at me as I went to find you. With the gun still in my hand, it went off in the scuffle. Into the air. He fell back to the ground, and I headed toward you."

It'd been five years ago. It was reasonable to assume that he might forget minor details about that night after so much time had passed. Still, Kenzie didn't trust Justin. The banging behind them became pounding. Suddenly, someone kicked the door hard enough that the metal bowed outward at the lock, and the door swung open.

One of the musicians stood in the doorway, his chest heaving with the effort. Kenzie didn't know whether to be relieved or scared.

"This is a private party. Who the fuck invited you?" Justin asked.

The man ran toward them, his jewel-encrusted mask still on his face. Justin was so surprised that he froze. The musician, who was a bigger man, hit Justin twice in the face so hard that Kenzie was afraid he'd be spitting out his teeth. She covered her mouth with her hands and stared as Justin stumbled back, blood dripping from his hands, now covering his face.

The masked musician stood there huffing in fury, his tattooed hands still balled into fists. "You!" the masked man screamed. "Don't go near her ever again."

Was this stranger protecting her? The musician pulled off his mask, and Kenzie saw the jagged scar along his left cheek. He swung his green eyes toward her.

Travis.

She screamed, and the world went black.

CHAPTER 33

When Kenzie came to, she was being carried down the street in the cold. The back of her head hurt. She must have hit it when she fainted. Justin held her in his arms as he hurried away from the hotel. He was breathing hard as if he'd been running with her.

"What happened?" she asked. "And Travis?" She whimpered at the memory of seeing him standing there only a few feet away from her. Breathing. Living. Fuming.

With a bloody nose and face already bruising, Justin shook his head. "He just won't die. He's like a fucking slasher villain—he keeps coming back again and again. Can you stand?" Concern creased his brow as he assessed her.

Kenzie was still lightheaded, but she was okay. She nodded, and he set her on her feet so that he could open the passenger door to a car. She was embarrassed that she'd fainted, but for a moment, she'd been looking at a dead man. The suddenness of it had been too much.

Justin held onto her arm again. He looked past her shoulder down the street, and she followed his gaze. No one came after them. "I took you out a back door. I didn't want the media getting a hold of this. Of us."

"What happened on the roof after I fainted?"

"Get in, please. I'll tell you everything as soon as I know we're away from here safely," he said. He urged her in with his hand against her back, and she stepped into the car. She looked back down the street once more before he closed her door.

Kenzie frowned. She didn't know if she should trust Justin. She barely knew him anymore.

As Justin pulled away from the curb, she realized she no longer had her clutch in her hand, which meant no phone. It must have fallen on the rooftop. A knot in her stomach formed. She had no way of calling for help if she needed it.

Justin sped through town. "I'm so sorry, Kenzie. I can't believe that he made it out of that house alive. I was *sure*..."

A lump formed in her throat. Kenzie watched the road, but she was reliving the horror of that night.

"I won't let him get to you again. I promise." Justin squeezed her hand reassuringly and returned his grip to the steering wheel. He genuinely seemed concerned for her welfare.

Maybe she'd gotten everything wrong. At only nineteen, had she been too gullible? Was the passion she'd felt with Travis completely one-sided, blinding her to reality?

Kenzie thought of the purple rose he'd given her and of him playing his cello for her. As she remembered the tenderness with which he'd touched her that last night together, she shook her head, unable to reconcile her memories of him with the monster that Justin made him out to be. Maybe she was still naïve. "Are you taking me home?"

"Don't you think if he knew about the event you were at, he'd also know where you live?"

"Maybe it was a coincidence that he was there. Isn't that possible?"

Kenzie thought back to the night she'd seen the Lamborghini Miura on the street outside her apartment. She'd tried to deny that it could be him, but Travis had probably been watching her for weeks now.

"It's going to be okay," Justin said. "I know a place where we can lay low for a bit. I want to make sure you're safe."

"Thank you," Kenzie murmured. Her mind was racing a mile a minute. Was he being sincere? She wasn't sure. If Justin took her someplace where she could get to a phone, she could call Sonja or even the police, if it came to it. The last thing she wanted, if Justin really was as dangerous as Travis had always claimed, was to make him angry on the highway. They were heading out of the city, and the landscape was turning increasingly rural. "Where are we going? I'm not familiar with this area."

"I've got a cabin out here on Muddy Bend Lake. It's not far out of the city. We'll be there in a few more minutes."

Though he kept reassuring her and gave her no reason to doubt him, she had that feeling, that danger radar going off in her brain that made her want to bolt. But there was nowhere to go. Kenzie paid close attention to the roads they took in case she ended up having to get away on foot. If she had something better than heels on, she could bail as soon as he parked the car. She wouldn't get very far barefooted, though.

"I need to call my friend Sonja. She's at the event. She'll be worried about me disappearing."

"Oh, I met Sonja earlier." He slowed the car. "Yeah, the signal isn't great out here. I've got a phone at the cabin, though. You're welcome to use it," Justin said as he pulled into a driveway.

That eased her mind. At least *someone* would know where she was tonight.

Justin got out and ran around the front of the car to open her door. The cabin in front of them was dark, a hulking figure with a shimmering lake behind it. The wind picked up and blew leaves across the yard. Kenzie followed him up the front porch and waited behind him as Justin unlocked the front door. As she entered the cabin, he flipped a light switch, illuminating a large living room, complete with a fireplace and a big sectional sofa dominating the room. To her right, a bar opened up into a large kitchen. This cabin was fancier than she'd imagined. She'd thought it would be small and quaint. She remembered enough about Justin, though, to realize how silly a notion that was. Justin Reese Greyer did nothing half-assed.

"How many rooms does this place have?" she asked.

Justin grinned. "Two downstairs and four upstairs. Plus a game room, sauna, and a theater in the basement."

"You've really done well for yourself, huh?"

Justin punched in a code to engage the security system. "I can't complain. I took a chance with Greyer Tech, and it paid off." He moved to the thermostat and turned on the heat.

She heard it hum as it came on, and she shivered in anticipation of warmth.

Drops of blood from the hit to his face earlier, no doubt, spattered the gold vest beneath his tux. "I didn't want to go into aerospace like my father. I wanted my own thing," he said as he walked to the fridge and opened it. "Water?"

"Sure," Kenzie said.

Justin unscrewed the top but left it on. She took the bottle but didn't drink it right away. The cold felt good in her hands despite the chill in the cabin. How was Justin so calm after being attacked on the roof of the hotel? Kenzie was still wound up and uneasy.

Justin pulled open a drawer, grabbed a dish towel, and filled it with ice. He put it gingerly on his swollen and bruised jaw. He held it there for a few moments before he moved it to his nose.

"You never told me what happened on the roof."

"Well, you fainted after he hit me." He moved the ice back to his jaw and winced. "He was screaming about you being his. We fought, which is when he busted my jaw. I hit him, and he fell forward and cracked his head against the parapet. It must have knocked him out, which is a good thing because it could have gotten much worse up there. I didn't wait for him to wake up. Unfortunately, I didn't have a weapon in my tux." He lowered the ice pack and gave her a sardonic smile, which bordered on monstrous with his swelling jaw and purple skin. "I scooped you up and got you out of there. I thought that getting you away from him was more important than getting the police involved in an assault case."

Kenzie nodded and sipped the water. "I just don't know why, after all this time, he'd contact me now. And why at the masquerade?"

"Maybe he wanted to catch you off guard. We may never understand his reasoning," he said to dismiss the conversation. Justin turned and dropped the ice pack into the sink. "Try not to worry about it. This place is secure, and I have a camera on the exterior that'll alert me to movement outside." Even so, he walked to the front window and took a peek. "I bought this place about a year ago and renovated it. Want a quick tour?"

Kenzie wanted to call Sonja, but she didn't want to seem ungrateful or uninterested. She'd insist on using his house phone as soon as they toured the cabin.

Justin pointed to the staircase. "That's where the guest bedrooms are. I won't make you climb the stairs in your heels. Around this corner is the game room." He opened a door to a long room with a billiards table, gaming chairs, and a gaming console attached to a large TV. She spotted a small karaoke setup in one corner and a mini-bar with a couple of stools. The room was painted dark gray, and everything looked brand new.

"Nice," she said.

"I haven't gotten to use it much," he said, closing the door. "I work a shit ton of hours. The sauna is at the end of the hall down there, and there's one guest bedroom beside it." He turned around and led her back to the living room. "The master bedroom is on the other side of the living room over there, and this is where the theater is." He gestured toward a door. "Come check it out. It's got plush theater seats, surround sound, a popcorn machine—basically everything you could want in a home theater."

Justin seemed genuinely excited to show off the features of his home. She wondered if he'd hosted any guests here yet. He opened the door and headed down a dark staircase. Kenzie followed. She had to slide her hand along the wall to keep from pitching forward. In the dim light, she felt a bit of vertigo. "You need a light for these stairs."

"True. I'll end up breaking my neck if I don't put some kind of light in soon. The laundry is down here, too," he said, motioning to a door behind him. He opened the door in front of him and gestured for her to go inside.

Kenzie took a step into the darkness.

"Let me get the light," he said, bumping into her and pushing her forward as he moved to search for the light switch on the wall.

The door behind them clicked shut, and lights illuminated the room.

Kenzie sucked in a breath. There was no theater here. Bare floors, a bed, and various bindings hung from the low ceiling. She blinked in confusion. Two oblong windows with bars along the opposite wall. A small commode and an open shower in the corner. Cameras in two corners near the ceiling. A prison.

Kenzie took in all these details in a matter of a few seconds before she turned to run. She slammed into Justin's chest as his open arms surrounded her.

"Where're you going, Kenzie?" He held her tight.

"Please," she said. Tears sprang to her eyes. *Stupid, stupid, stupid*, she chastised herself.

"Oh, you'll beg." A smile teased the corners of his mouth, but his eyes lit up with wicked delight. "It's a little early for that, though." Justin pushed her backward with such force that she fell on her ass. She dropped the water bottle, which bounced across the concrete and rolled to a stop. "I've been waiting for this day for years. You're the one who got away, but now, I've got you back. I have it all, but you're all I want."

Those were the kind of words every woman dreamed of hearing, but not from someone who'd lost their fucking mind. Kenzie whimpered. Despite the adrenaline now pumping through her body, she felt tired and dizzy. Instead of trying to sit up, she lay back against the cold floor, her eyes resting on the water bottle that'd rolled away. He must have put something in it. Maybe it was laced with something before they'd come here. Her mind continued reeling even as her body stilled.

Justin had obviously thought this out in great detail. His plan was to imprison her all along, even before Travis showed back up. Maybe he'd even acquired Dillon Books because of her. She felt sick. All he'd said about Travis was bullshit. He'd fed her lies to confuse her.

Kenzie's eyes closed. Too heavy. Too tired.

"Go to sleep, sweetheart." His voice was only an echo in her well of despair.

CHAPTER 34

Travis winced as he touched his head and rolled over. That psychotic motherfucker had gotten lucky again, and this time, it might cost Kenzie her life. Despite the pounding in his head, he sat up; he'd endure any pain to get to her. He placed the mask back on his face and headed down to the ballroom, degrading himself the entire time for not killing Justin years ago.

His friend Ben had gotten him the quartet gig and was playing in his place on the stage as six of them had come to relieve each other for breaks at the end of every other set. Travis cut through the people without stopping to tell Ben where he was going. He had to get to Kenzie and fast. He'd seen the kinds of things Justin was capable of, and it was harrowing.

In another few minutes, he ran along the street and headed toward the parking garage where he'd left his car. When he got into the Lamborghini, he paused, wincing as the pounding in his head reached a deafening drum beat that made his head throb with each pulse of his blood. He thought he might vomit, and he willed the pain in his head to cease. He was certain he was concussed.

Travis pulled up the tracking app on his phone to determine where Justin had taken her. He'd placed a tracking device under Justin's car yesterday while the guy was out doing God knows what with the woman he'd held hostage in his apartment for days—the apartment he'd recently acquired near Kenzie's building.

Travis hadn't found where Justin was staying until the night he followed Justin from Kenzie's visit with Mark. He watched Justin closely then. Over the past few years, Travis had noticed a pattern: missing women who were later found burned or submerged in rivers and lakes—incidents that often coincided with Justin's whereabouts at the time of their deaths. Travis suspected he was killing them, but he had no proof. He felt sick to his stomach for not being able to save the latest woman who'd gone missing. She'd left behind a husband and a three-year-old child. Fucking sick prick.

The app showed Justin still en route, though already out of the city.

Fuck.

Travis squeezed his eyes shut for a moment before he put the car in reverse and backed out.

Travis thought he'd had everything planned out so that the police would catch Justin finally. He'd taken video of Justin leaving with the luggage and getting into the car that he'd later set on fire. When they realized the charred remains were the woman who'd gone missing, Travis could send in the footage anonymously. Surely, some of the woman's DNA would be found inside that apartment. That would be enough for them to look at similar body disposals and cross-reference them to when Justin had been in the vicinity of the murders.

Travis decided long ago that revealing himself to Kenzie would put her in danger. If Justin suspected that Kenzie and Travis could be together, he'd ruin it out of spite. He hadn't figured out Travis was alive—of that, Travis was certain—but Justin had an unhealthy obsession with Kenzie, it seemed. And he had a proclivity for killing women. Sometimes men, too.

Travis hoped Justin's arrival to the city was a coincidence, but he knew now that it was intentional. Travis had tried so hard to be a better man, the kind of man Kenzie wanted him to be, instead of seeking his own justice. That was over now. Travis was going to flay that bastard. If he laid one fucking finger on Kenzie, he'd torture Justin and laugh the entire time that bastard cried and screamed. His hands tightened around the steering wheel. In fact, he looked forward to it.

Travis tried so hard to do right by her. He'd watched her over the years and protected her every chance he could get, though she'd never known. One night, not long after she'd moved to the city, he'd stopped a guy from mugging her. She hadn't even noticed the thief stalking her. He'd pounded the guy's face in, but Travis had left him breathing.

He'd even followed Mark around for a while to make sure the guy was on the up and up. No way was he letting some asshole hurt her. Mark had been good to her, as much as it hurt Travis to watch it play out. He was beginning to think Mark would be the *one* for her, and the possibility of it tore him apart. She deserved to be happy, but that didn't mean that Travis had to like it.

No more playing nice. No more taking the fucking high road.

Travis was done running away from his problems. And he was done avoiding the one woman who'd truly made him happy, even if only for a short while.

With murder on his mind, he peeled tires as he exited the parking garage and headed toward the psychopath and the love of his life.

CHAPTER 35

When Kenzie came to, she found herself bound by her wrists and ankles to the bed in the basement. Her eyes searched the room for Justin, though her head was still foggy. He'd taken off her dress, but she still had on her bra and panties. She pulled at her restraints, but they didn't budge. She looked at the camera, pointed straight at her.

"Let me outta here!" she screamed. Maybe she should have been scared, but she was angry.

What did he think he was doing? Did he really believe that he could win Kenzie's affection by imprisoning her down here? Or was he just toying with her until he killed her for knowing too much? Lies had slipped out of his mouth as easily as the truth. She couldn't take anything he said as fact.

Kenzie tried to shake away the fuzziness of whatever he'd given her. She licked her dry lips.

Kenzie heard a key turn in the lock, and the door opened. Her heart pounded as her courage disappeared. Justin stepped inside the room. He'd showered and changed into jeans. Water still dripped from his dark hair. He looked like the college hottie she had a crush on years ago. Except, now she knew he was fucking nuts.

"You woke up quicker than I expected. You must not have had much of the water I laced with chloral hydrate. It's so easy to get Mickey Finn on the streets."

"Why do you have me tied up, Justin?" Kenzie asked through gritted teeth.

"By the look on your face, I think you'd probably try to gouge my eyeballs out right now. If you're restrained, I have your undivided attention."

"You lied to me. You imprisoned me. I don't want to hear anything you say."

Justin turned his back to her. He picked up a knife. "Oh, you will. You see, I know you like some dark shit if you were fucking Travis. So what are your kinks, Kenzie? What do I have to do for you to ride me like you rode that Mark fucker?"

Kenzie narrowed her eyes. "What do you know about Mark?"

Had Justin killed Mark? Or had Travis? Were Justin and Travis very different from each other? She didn't know anymore.

Justin walked to the bed, his eyes roaming over her body appreciatively. He touched her mound through her panties, and she tried to jerk away, but the restraints wouldn't allow her to move even an inch. She turned her face from him.

"You fucking look at me!" he screamed. He bent down and put the scalpel next to her face. "You keep your eyes on me, or I'll cut them out."

He's fucking crazy, she thought. The realization that he was going to kill her hit her, and she broke out in a cold sweat. There was no way out for her. She tried to keep herself from trembling. She didn't want to show him her fear.

His features softened. He gently moved a lock of hair from her jaw. "You are so beautiful." His thumb grazed her bottom lip. "I don't want to hurt you, Kenzie. I don't. I want to give you everything. I want to worship every inch of your skin. I want to know what you taste like. I want to feel the warmth of your insides. I want to give you pleasures you never thought possible, but there's something you need to know and accept before we can be together. I'm a monster with women other than you. I won't stop. I can't." His voice broke.

Justin took the scalpel and cut off her panties as she held her breath, so afraid that he was going to nick her skin with the sharp blade. He yanked the material from underneath her and tossed it on the floor.

"I'm ready to see that pretty cunt weep."

Justin laid down the scalpel and picked up a tiny remote. He clicked a button, and a vibration started deep within her pussy, rising in intensity. Her eyes widened as she squirmed. He must have inserted a bullet vibrator into her while she'd been knocked out. He clicked the remote again, and the pattern of pulsation changed, giving her pussy waves of pleasure. Beads of sweat popped out on her forehead and upper lip as she fought for control.

"I want to hear you come. Over and over. And when you're delirious with lust, you'll know how I feel when I hunt." He watched her intently as he changed the motion again.

Kenzie breathed harder, insistent pulses, trying to dissociate herself from the pleasure. The pulses sped up inside her, and she squirmed again, trying to press her pelvis forward, but that only increased the pleasure. She cried out before biting off the sound, refusing to come for him. Her body betrayed her, though.

Soon, she was rocking her pelvis back and forth, trying so hard not to come. He changed the pattern of pulses again, and it felt like lightning zapping her deep in her core. Her eyes rolled back as her head fell back, and she bucked her hips in the air before her body went stiff with a staggering orgasm. She didn't realize she was screaming until it was nearly over, and the pulsing stopped. Her whole body shook with the effort.

"Beautiful," he murmured. "We're just warming up." He took the scalpel and cut her bra in two while Kenzie lay there, exhausted. Justin licked at a nipple as he swirled a finger in her soaked pussy. Then, he sucked her wetness from his finger. "I can't wait to stick my entire face between your legs and pleasure you, sweetheart."

Kenzie shook her head, but her mind was so foggy. When the pulsation began again, she wailed, and this time, she came much faster. She didn't have the stamina to fight it anymore.

"Now, you're starting to understand. Yes?"

Kenzie nodded. She'd do whatever it took for him to stop this insanity. Tears rolled down her temples and into her hair. "Please, stop."

"I want you to understand me, Kenzie. I think you're the only woman in the world who could love me for the messed-up monster of a man that I am."

I'll never love you, she thought. "I understand," she said. *That you're a devil.*

"Hmm, I don't think you do yet. But you will."

Justin clicked the remote again.

CHAPTER 36

Travis parked down the road and used the cover of night to his advantage. He sheathed a blade in his boot and a smaller knife in his pocket. He took off his jacket and vest. They would only restrict his movements. The white shirt would give him away in the darkness, so he removed it, too. Perhaps the tattoos he'd gotten over the past few years would give him a measure of camouflage in the darkness. The tattoos had been his only outlet for the frustration of what he'd gone through after he left his old life and Kenzie behind.

Just when Travis thought he was becoming somewhat human again, Justin turned him right back into the monster that he had become when he met Kenzie. She'd never be able to love him. He'd be alone forever—or until he refused to live in loneliness anymore.

But one thing was for certain—he'd end this tonight.

He moved silently through the trees toward the yard where the cabin was lit up in the dark night, its lights a blurry reflection on the lake to his left. He knew that he'd trip a security system sensor. There was no way someone with

Justin's money and tech experience would leave his home unprotected, especially when that somebody had a helluva lot to hide. Travis would have to be ready to fight when it happened.

Travis was more than ready to fight, though. He was ready to slaughter that motherfucker. Adrenaline flooded his system as he ran toward the house. Instead of trying to get through the front door, he picked up a wrought-iron chair from the front porch and threw it against a window. It cracked the glass with a loud bang before falling to the porch. He grabbed it and swung again, using all his strength, and the chair crashed into the house. He kicked shards of glass away before climbing into the living room.

No one came running, and he raised an eyebrow. Fear settled into his chest. That could mean that the psycho was far too busy with Kenzie to notice, and Travis' blood boiled as he tore through the house searching for them. He ran upstairs first, but found only empty bedrooms. Then, he searched the first floor. Still no sign of them. Had the guy ditched the car and taken her somewhere else? Travis hoped to hell not because he'd never find them if Justin did.

Travis stood in the living room, trying to slow his breathing and calm his pounding heart. He shut his eyes and listened. When the hum of the HVAC went off, the silence was deeper, and he thought he heard the faintest scream. He turned his head to listen. Or was it his imagination?

Travis wrenched open the only door he hadn't tried on this floor. A dark gaping maw led deep into the basement. Without hesitation, he fled down the steps, reaching in front of him for a door or wall. Down here, he heard it clearer—crying and moaning. The sense of urgency flooding through him made him want to jump out of his skin. Travis followed the sound to his left and tried the knob, which was locked. He backed up to the door behind him and then kicked at the door in front of him with as much force as he could muster. With a guttural howl of rage, he fell through the splintered door, hit the floor, and rolled into a crouched position.

Travis took in the scene before him even as he reached for the knife in his boot. Kenzie lay on a bed, naked, out of her mind, and sobbing while Justin scrambled for something to attack the intruder with and defend his monstrous deeds. The heady scent of Kenzie filled the room.

As Travis straightened, Justin grunted and plowed toward him, a scalpel in his hand. Justin's movements were wild; Travis could use that to his advantage. As Travis jabbed at Justin's stomach with his own knife, Justin turned. The knife glanced off the side of his torso, and blood blossomed on his skin as he brought the scalpel down, slashing into Travis' forearm. Travis kicked at Justin's kneecap, which made him buckle to the floor.

Justin screwed up his face. "Why won't you die?" Justin asked through clenched teeth, spittle flying from his mouth as Travis kicked the scalpel from his hand. Justin turned over to reach for the scalpel, and Travis brought the knife down so hard at Justin's back that the blade's tip hit the concrete beneath him.

Travis pulled out the knife and wiped the blood on his tux pants before hurrying over to Kenzie. Her blonde hair was ringing with sweat, and a sheen of sweat covered her body, but despite that, she shivered. Was she in shock?

"What has he fucking done to you, vixen?" he asked tenderly. She looked so fragile, he was afraid to even touch her.

Kenzie's eyes finally focused on him, and her eyebrows turned up questioningly. Then, her face crumbled as she cried sobs that caught in her throat and wracked her body. "Get it out," she whispered.

At first, Travis couldn't tell what she'd said. For a moment, he thought she was telling him to leave.

Louder, Kenzie said, "Please. Get it out of me." Her plea was so piteous that it broke his heart.

What could she mean? What had Justin put in her? Travis frowned as his eyes swept her body. "Oh, fuck." He moved to the end of the bed and peered between her legs. Justin must have put something inside her pussy or her ass, but Travis couldn't tell. She was so swollen and red. "Here?" he asked with a gesture, and she nodded. "Okay," he said as he came back to the head of the bed. "Here's what I'm going to do. I'm going to cut your bindings, and then I'll remove them. Hold perfectly still for me, baby."

Kenzie nodded. Her crying had tapered off, and she stilled her body as he cut through the straps.

Travis laid down the knife and gripped the side of the bed for a moment. "That motherfucker," he muttered. Her eyes were so wide and bloodshot. He knelt and pressed his index finger inside her. A little ways in, he felt the metal of whatever Justin had shoved there. She was drenched, so there was plentiful lubrication. She clenched in discomfort, though. Fucking trauma, no doubt. "Is it a vibrator?"

The thought of Justin touching her there drove him insane with rage.

When she nodded, he said, "Relax, Kenzie. I have to get two fingers on it, and then I'm going to tug gently, okay? And when I do, I want you to push it."

She nodded but grasped his wrist as if she didn't believe him. He pressed his lips to her fingers and then pushed in his thumb. She tightened her grip on his wrist. One little tug with the help of her own internal muscles pushing it out, and the bullet vibrator slid out.

Travis tossed it on the bed and gathered Kenzie into his arms. She still shivered, but she embraced him back, which he took as a good sign.

As she clung to him, her fingers tightened until they dug into his back. She took in a ragged gasp, and Travis turned. Justin stood up behind him. Blood covered his shirt, and he swayed where he stood. The look on his pale face was pure madness.

Travis pushed Kenzie back as he grabbed for his knife. A second too late, Justin gripped the blade and held it toward Travis.

"I fucking hate you," Justin said, but with the word 'hate' came a string of blood from his mouth.

Travis grabbed the vibrator and launched himself at Justin, who was thrown back and landed hard on the floor. The knife skidded across the concrete. Travis said, "Go to hell, you fucking monster," and shoved the vibrator in Justin's mouth so hard that he broke a few teeth. Travis punched him in the mouth and then punched him in the torso, where the blood covered his shirt. He kept punching until he was too tired to make another hit. Then, he pulled his second knife from his pocket and slit Justin's throat for good measure. "Let him get up now."

Travis sat on top of Justin's lifeless body, his chest heaving with the effort and his fists bloody. As the rage subsided and his breathing calmed, he realized he heard a strange noise from Justin's face. He frowned and leaned forward. Buzzing.

Travis turned to see Kenzie sitting up on the bed, her hair a mess and her eyes wild. She held a remote in her hand, and she was smiling.

CHAPTER 37
A Week Later

An early snow blanketed the city in a fine white dusting. Kenzie stood at her window and watched the large, falling flakes. Kenzie hadn't gone back to work, but she knew she needed to resume life soon. She had healing to do, but part of that healing meant trying to get back into a normal routine.

The worst part about going back to the office would be the looks of pity. No, what would be worse than that, she decided, would be those who refused to look at her at all, as if she was now tainted somehow, as if by her sheer interaction with the monster, she'd become one, too. She rubbed her hands against her arms. Or maybe she was exaggerating their reactions in her mind—and anticipating the worst.

Kenzie looked down at the empty street. News reporters had been camped out beneath her apartment windows for days, but the snow had finally driven them away. Her parents had visited for the first few days to make sure she was okay. Sonja brought her some groceries a couple of days ago so Kenzie wouldn't have to face the media, or anyone for that matter, right now. She planned to tell her story, but it'd be on her terms and when she was ready.

Detective Lincoln came by yesterday to ask a few follow-up questions. This time, he hadn't been so condescending, and she'd appreciated the effort.

Justin's very own video footage helped police see what a monster he was and that he'd been responsible for other deaths by his own admission to Kenzie. She hated they had footage of what he'd done to her, though. It made her sick and even more violated to think about it. Detective Lincoln said that they'd already posthumously linked him to eight other killings, but in reality, there were probably twice that many. It turned out that Justin liked to keep videos of his victims, though they'd been hidden in files on his computer.

The Greyer family, who now owned the Greyer Tech corporation, were trying their damnedest to hush it up, but Kenzie vowed to tell her story, no matter if it cost her the editing position with Dillon Books. What Justin had done to women was atrocious, and money wasn't going to cover his evil any longer.

A light knock at the door pulled her from her thoughts. Kenzie opened the door, and Travis smiled down at her. His forearm was still bandaged, but he looked calm and healthy, otherwise. Not like he'd recently fought off a serial killer and saved her life.

"Hey, vixen." Travis wrapped her in a tender hug.

Kenzie clung to him as he kicked the door closed behind him. His arms felt so comforting. She wanted to be held like that forever.

"Sorry to just now be coming by. It's been a fuck ton of work trying to get everything straightened out."

Kenzie released him and nodded. She reached around him and locked the door. "Want some coffee or cocoa before we sit down?"

Travis looked at her warily. "Cocoa. Extra marshmallows."

She knew he expected what was coming. They hadn't gotten a free moment alone since that night. He'd been in the hospital getting himself stitched up, and she'd been there, too, being assessed by doctors, and the bastards wouldn't let him in her room to hold her and keep her safe, something she'd wanted as much as he did, but they'd denied contact for a while. Then, they'd both spent many hours being questioned by the police after being released from the hospital. They'd questioned Travis much longer. He was a dead man, after all.

Kenzie busied herself with heating the kettle of water. "Did you know that I saw your car a few weeks before?"

Travis stuffed his hands into his jeans pockets and watched her.

"I thought I was losing my mind," she said with a huff of what was supposed to be laughter that didn't quite make it. It was an agitated sound, and she winced. She didn't want to be frustrated with him, but she was.

"I was watching you, trying to keep you safe. I'd been watching you for five whole years, off and on, when I could, more so in the beginning than lately." He paused and measured his words. "You seemed to be doing fine. More than fine. A career, your own place, a boyfriend."

Kenzie looked up from where she was stirring the cocoa. She wasn't sure if he'd known about Mark. Apparently, he had, and she felt a pang of regret. "I'm sorry. I—"

"What for? For all you knew, I was dead, and I let you believe that. You have nothing to be sorry for. I don't fault you, vixen. I didn't think you'd go all these years without intimacy."

But she would've. If she'd only known. If she'd had a hint that he was out there, she wouldn't have looked at another man.

Kenzie dropped a handful of marshmallows into each mug and brought them to the coffee table. Before sitting, she turned to him. She wanted to ask him about the murders on campus five years ago, but she was so paranoid that someone might hear, that her apartment was bugged or something, that she didn't dare utter the questions she'd been thinking about for so long. She knew that he'd killed Vaughn, and she'd heard him admit to killing Sam. But now, she wondered if the others—the frat brother Caleb, who'd been murdered outside his girlfriend's sorority, and the female who'd been found near campus burned—had been Justin's victims. Instead, she sat and patted the couch beside her.

Did the past matter? Hadn't Travis tried to explain why he'd done what he'd done? Did vengeance make it right? He'd redeemed himself in her eyes when he delivered her from the hands of a monster, no matter what society would say about it. And she'd keep his secrets. She only hoped that his proclivity for violent retaliation was dead and buried.

"How did you know where to find us? We were in the middle of nowhere. I was sure I'd be dead before anyone found me."

"Tracking device. I put it on his car when I saw him carry the luggage full of his latest victim and take off in a hot car. He was accelerating with her, and I knew he was going to get another victim soon. The fact that he'd moved to your city led me to believe that he'd target you eventually," Travis said.

"Why didn't you come find me after the fire? Why did you let me think you were dead and that Justin had killed you?"

"I was trying to protect you. When I saw that he wasn't going to come after you for what you knew, I left. I didn't want you to be weighed down by my burdens, and I certainly didn't want him targeting you because of me showing back up.

"He used my indecision and inaction against me. I should have gone after him and killed him before he could ever get to us. God, I wish I had. That was my mistake. I underestimated him. I didn't exactly know what he was capable of or the amount of depravity in his soul. And you suffered for it."

They both sat in silence for a moment, lost in their thoughts.

Travis took a sip of the cocoa, and he licked a bit of melted marshmallow from his lip. Kenzie took it as another good sign—that simple flick of his tongue made her want to taste him again.

Travis said, "I felt like he had to be here for you. It was too much of a coincidence. I took the gig with the quartet because I found out he was going to be there. I'd played some other gigs with them, and I wanted to watch him. But I didn't know you were at the masquerade, not until I ran into you before you went up to the roof. When you spoke, that's when I knew, and I was so floored by the realization that he already had you in his grasp that I hesitated. I fucking hesitated *again*."

Kenzie shook her head. He was blaming himself. "It's not your fault."

"I feel responsible for *all* these deaths. If I'd taken care of him back in college, he wouldn't have hurt so many people. He wouldn't have come after you. I failed."

Kenzie cupped Travis' jaw in her hand, the scars that ran along his face beneath her fingertips. "No, you're only human. You aren't a monster hellbent on only one goal. You felt, you loved, you made mistakes. Those things aren't weaknesses." She took his hands in hers, and she realized that one tattoo that snaked up his arm was a depiction of Frankenstein's bride. Kenzie smiled. "I wish you'd stayed."

"With what was going on around campus back then, I quickly realized I'd go down for it. I knew how it looked, and if Justin could pin all of it on me, he would. So I took the chance I had when he set my house on fire. I waited until everyone had cleared out after the arson investigation. When they said that I'd probably died in that fire and cleared out, I changed the battery in my dad's car and got it out of the barn, and I hit the road. I wandered aimlessly for a while. I didn't know what to do with myself. By the time I got back into town to look for you, you'd left. And you didn't make it easy to track you down. So much of your life had changed, too. You were finishing up college in the city, and you had your own apartment. You looked... happy. I didn't want to screw that up for you."

"You wouldn't have. Your absence did more damage than your presence would have." She squeezed his hand. "I missed you *so* much."

He shook his head, and tears glimmered in his green eyes. "I wanted so badly to be the man that you wanted me to be."

"You are, Travis." She pressed her lips softly against his. "You're not the villain in this story. You're the hero."

Travis wrapped her in a hug. She wished he was here every night to hold her and make her feel safe again.

Kenzie was afraid of his answer, but she had to ask. "Are you going to disappear again? Or will you stay?"

Travis pulled back and looked at her as if he were trying to remember every inch of her face. He smoothed a lock of hair behind her ear. "I've got to come back from the dead first."

EPILOGUE

A Year Later

Thunder shook the roof of the apartment building and rattled the windows. The rain looked like it was blowing sideways outside. Kenzie pulled her thick sweatshirt over her head to chase away the chill from the storm, and she settled back down on her couch to watch a scary movie. She was in the mood for something obscure or something from her childhood, maybe. She searched through titles until she settled on the original Scream. It was one of her comfort movies.

After what she'd been through with her own serial killer stalker last year, one would think she'd detest movies like this. Her therapist said that for many who have dealt with trauma, watching scary movies was an empowering way to face fears while still feeling safe.

Or maybe she was a horror-loving weirdo, as Lena would have said. She smiled at the thought of her old friend.

Kenzie paused the movie—no way was she missing the Drew Barrymore opening—and put a bag of popcorn in the microwave to pop. She grabbed a bottle of water and a chocolate and toffee bar from her fridge. She poured the popcorn into a bowl and took the snack into the living room.

Thunder rumbled again, but she drowned it out with the sounds of the opening scene of the movie. Kenzie munched on popcorn and grinned at the television. She popped a rectangle of chocolate into her mouth as the phone in the movie rang, and Ghostface's familiar scratchy voice filled the room.

Lightning struck close enough that the pop of the jolt startled Kenzie, and she gasped as the lights flickered twice and went out. "Great, no TV, no internet, no heat." She sat still on the couch for a moment, letting her eyes adjust to the darkness and letting her pulse return to normal. Thankfully, she'd left a pumpkin cinnamon candle burning in her bedroom earlier, and it still flickered illumination down her hallway.

As she approached her bedroom, she saw that a dark figure blocked out most of the light. He was wearing a Frankenstein's monster mask.

Kenzie's tense shoulders relaxed. "You couldn't find anything more original than that?"

"You're the one watching Ghostface," Travis said. He pulled the mask off his head and replaced it.

Kenzie couldn't tell what it was in the dark. As the lightning lit up the bedroom where he stood, she saw it was a leering clown mask. Its white skin contrasted with its red hair and jagged yellow teeth.

The grin slid from her face. "You know how much I hate clowns!"

"You better run, then." Travis took off down the hallway, chasing her through the house.

She ran around the bar, and she thought he'd cornered her in the kitchen. She squeezed past him, spinning out of his grasp before he tackled her and threw her across the couch. He leaned down, the nose of the clown mask almost touching hers. In a deep, guttural voice, he said, "You've been a naughty girl, and I'm gonna make that pussy pay."

Travis' voice turned her into liquid. She appreciated that he still played with her this way because she didn't want to be handled like a delicate teacup ready to break. She wanted to be tossed around and handled like he'd done when they first met.

Travis turned her over, slapped her ass, and yanked down her jeans. "Are you getting wet yet for the killer clown?" He cackled as she screamed and wiggled away from him.

Kenzie turned over, the clown mask looming over her. He yanked the mask off his head and threw it across the living room. "That's better. Now, you can make my pussy pay." She grinned as she raised her eyebrows in a suggestive expression.

Travis hummed with interest as he slipped his fingers into her panties. A finger slid over her clit, and she shivered.

His green eyes twinkled in the darkness. He licked her jaw and lowered his lips to her ear. In a raspy whisper that rivaled Ghostface's measured, gravelly voice, Travis said, "I can't wait to bury myself balls deep inside of you."

CONTENT WARNINGS

Potential Triggers:
    explicit sexual scenes
    dubious consent bordering on non-consent
    consensual non-consent
    knife play
    choking
    biting
    voyeurism
    physical injuries/scars
    grief and loss depiction
    PTSD
    masked men
    suicide ideation
    murder
    serial killings
    rape
    sexual torture
    BDSM

female victimization
dismemberment

AFTERWORD

Thank you for reading this work of fiction. Please consider leaving a review or rating, which are appreciated on any and all platforms. If you enjoyed the story, please recommend this book to other readers.

You can find C. Cyan on Instagram @ccyanauthor and on Goodreads.

The Spotify playlist for *Dark Needs* can be found here: https://open.spotify.com/playlist/6FQ1qWij30zNgeb01Cbpix Or use this QR code to access the playlist.

Assistance:
If you have thoughts of suicide, help is available 24/7 and is free and confidential. In the U.S., call or text 988. Someone is there to listen. You don't have to struggle alone.

If someone is physically or emotionally abusing you, call 800.799.SAFE (7233) or text START to 88788 for help from the National Domestic Violence Hotline.

Made in the USA
Middletown, DE
18 January 2025